HOLIDAY Hope

Holiday Express Book 1
A Sweet Historical Holiday Romance
by
USA Today Bestselling Author
SHANNA HATFIELD

Holiday Hope
Holiday Express Series, Book 1

Copyright © 2021 by Shanna Hatfield

ISBN: 9798773855484

All rights reserved. By purchasing this publication through an authorized outlet, you have been granted the nonexclusive, nontransferable right to access and read the text of this book. No part of this publication may be reproduced, distributed, downloaded, decompiled, reverse engineered, transmitted, or stored in or introduced into any information storage and retrieval system, in any form or by any means, including photocopying, recording, or other electronic or mechanical methods, now known or hereafter invented, without the written permission of the author, except in the case of brief quotations embodied in reviews and certain other noncommercial uses permitted by copyright law. Please purchase only authorized editions.

For permission requests, please contact the author, with a subject line of "permission request" at the e-mail address below or through her website.
shanna@shannahatfield.com

This is a work of fiction. Names, characters, businesses, places, events, and incidents either are the product of the author's imagination or are used in a fictitious manner. Any resemblance to actual persons, living or dead, business establishments, or actual events is purely coincidental.

Cover Design: Covers and Cupcakes, LLC.

Published by Wholesome Hearts Publishing, LLC.
wholesomeheartspublishing@gmail.com

*To Cora
And all the young readers who
find adventures in books . . .*

Books by Shanna Hatfield

FICTION

CONTEMPORARY

Holiday Brides
Valentine Bride
Summer Bride
Easter Bride
Lilac Bride

Rodeo Romance
The Christmas Cowboy
Wrestlin' Christmas
Capturing Christmas
Barreling Through Christmas
Chasing Christmas
Racing Christmas
Keeping Christmas
Roping Christmas
Remembering Christmas

Grass Valley Cowboys
The Cowboy's Christmas Plan
The Cowboy's Spring Romance
The Cowboy's Summer Love
The Cowboy's Autumn Fall
The Cowboy's New Heart
The Cowboy's Last Goodbye

Summer Creek
Catching the Cowboy
Rescuing the Rancher
Protecting the Princess
Distracting the Deputy

Women of Tenacity
Heart of Clay
Heart of Hope
Heart of Love

HISTORICAL

Pendleton Petticoats
Dacey   *Lacey*
Aundy   *Bertie*
Caterina *Millie*
Ilsa   *Dally*
Marnie *Quinn*
          Evie

Pendleton Promises
Sadie

Baker City Brides
Tad's Treasure
Crumpets and Cowpies
Thimbles and Thistles
Corsets and Cuffs
Bobbins and Boots
Lightning and Lawmen
Dumplings and Dynamite

Hearts of the War
Garden of Her Heart
Home of Her Heart
Dream of Her Heart

Hardman Holidays
The Christmas Bargain
The Christmas Token
The Christmas Calamity
The Christmas Vow
The Christmas Quandary
The Christmas Confection
The Christmas Melody
The Christmas Ring
The Christmas Wish

Chapter One

1884

A bump in the track jostled Cora Lee Schuster from a restless slumber. Weary from days of travel across the great expanse of the United States, she hesitated to open her eyes and begin the day.

She'd climbed into the upper berth of the train car more than ready to rest last night, but sleep had proven elusive through the long midnight hours.

Plagued by thoughts of what her immediate future might hold when she arrived in Holiday, a newly constructed town in the wilds of Eastern Oregon, she found it impossible to relax and fully surrender to her dreams.

Had she been completely crazy to travel all the way from Cincinnati to marry a rancher? She supposed the answer to that question would become clear soon enough. By noon, the train would arrive in Holiday and she'd meet her intended, Jude Coleman. Would he be a man as gritty and tough as the images his name conjured in her mind? Or someone kind? Someone she could come to love?

Cora Lee drew in a deep breath, needing to clear her thoughts. Instead of a cleansing lungful of air, she inhaled a stale, sour odor that put her in mind of rancid cabbage. Nose wrinkled in disgust, she started to rise, only to find the braid she'd fashioned last night pinned down, prohibiting any movement.

Curious, she reached up and felt around the top of her pillow until her fingers encountered something both bony and hairy. A scream clawed upward in her throat as she envisioned a wild animal curled around her head. When the offending weight shifted, she squelched the urge to shriek and quickly sat up. She glanced over her shoulder to see two incredibly large, hairy feet resting in her berth.

Cora Lee rolled her eyes, then glanced down at a noise from the berth below her. Anne Charles, her newly acquainted friend, pressed a hand over her mouth to keep from bursting into laughter. When Cora Lee made a silly face, the two women could no longer hold back their humor. Cora Lee buried her face into the mattress while Anne held a pillow over her face.

Once their amusement subsided, Anne rolled to the edge of her berth and shook her head. "What a way to begin your day," she whispered.

"I thought something had crawled by my head and died," Cora Lee spoke in a hushed tone. "Maybe the fellow has passed on to glory and that's why his feet stink so much."

"Shh! He might hear you. At least, I hope that those gigantic things belong to a man. I'd hate to think of a woman having such enormous feet or hairy legs!"

Just then, the feet twitched, and the owner pulled them back inside his berth, causing the two women to laugh again.

"We might as well get ready for the day," Anne said, reaching beneath her berth and handing Cora Lee her satchel.

"Agreed. If we hurry, we might even beat the line to the lavatory," Cora Lee said, hurrying to dress in the cramped quarters. Hastily changing from her nightgown into a traveling dress that would forever be embedded with soot from the coal that powered the train down the track, she sat cross-legged on the bed, combing her hair, her mouth full of hairpins. The train lurched around a curve, throwing her off balance. She spewed the hairpins onto her lap, lest she swallow them. Grasping onto the berth brace kept her from shooting right off the bed, but her traveling companion didn't fare as well.

Anne squealed as she was thrown out of her berth into the center aisle, landing on her backside with her dress slipping down one shoulder.

Cora Lee shoved the pins into her hair, hopped off the berth, and stepped between Anne and two interested-appearing men dressed in western garb as they moved closer. She held a hand out to Anne, helped her to her feet, then pushed her back behind the curtain surrounding their berth. With a curt nod to the men, she followed Anne into the bit of privacy afforded by the curtain and helped to right the woman's rumpled clothing.

"Well, that's one way to get the blood flowing

first thing," Cora Lee said with a smile.

"I am mortified!" Anne hissed. Her entire face was a bright shade of pink as she smoothed her dress, then nervously fussed with her hair.

"Don't be. At least you didn't have smelly feet next to your face."

Anne's tense shoulders relaxed slightly. "True. I only fell into the midst of the car with men ogling me from every direction," she said with a hint of sarcasm.

"Oh, it wasn't nearly that dramatic." Cora Lee took the brush from Anne and gave the woman's luxuriant brown hair several strokes before fashioning it into the high pompadour her friend favored. "There. All ready."

"Perhaps those who were awake returned to sleep," Anne said as they pulled back the curtains and stepped into the aisle.

"Or it could be everyone was awakened by our jolting ride," Cora Lee said, leading the way to the lavatory. At least they were fortunate to be traveling in a car that had a lavatory for ladies and another for gentlemen. In fact, Cora Lee had been both surprised and amazed by how nice her accommodations had been the entire trip. She'd half-anticipated traveling in the immigrant car, but for the most part, she'd been comfortable and well-fed.

As she and Anne waited for a turn in the lavatory, she glanced at the woman with whom she'd felt an immediate kinship. They'd met in Omaha while they were waiting to board the train that would carry them west. Anne was a proper

Englishwoman. She'd arrived in America a year ago with her maidenly aunt. The woman had passed not long after they'd settled into a small home in New York City. It had taken Anne months to sort through the paperwork, only to discover the woman who was also her guardian had left her penniless. Unable to find suitable work, Anne had decided to take a chance on the unknown and become a mail-order bride.

Cora Lee could well relate to Anne and her story of being forced to make a choice between poverty, working in a deplorable job, or accepting an offer of marriage from a complete stranger. The idea of marriage seemed far more palatable than the other options, so here she was on her way to Holiday.

The discovery that Holiday was also Anne's destination nearly made her weep with joy. Anne had agreed to wed the owner of the local livery and blacksmith shop. Cora Lee could hardly envision the petite, elegant Anne married to some hulking brute who smelled of sweat, iron, and horses, but she hoped her friend would find happiness in the unconventional union.

Cora Lee contemplated her own impending marriage to a man she didn't know. The last letter she'd received from Jude had said he'd give her time to get acclimated to ranch life before they wed. At least she wouldn't be immediately pressed into the role of a wife.

She knew from Jude's letters that he resided on Elk Creek Ranch, just north of town. He, along with his father and brother, raised beef cattle and also trained horses they sold to the military. Jude had also mentioned their property included timber, so she assumed the town had to be in the mountains or close to them.

She'd never heard of Holiday before she'd answered Jude's advertisement for a wife. She'd even attempted to locate the town on a map, but it had only been founded six years prior when a large gold strike drew men to the area. Now that money poured into town from the mine, respectable businesses had been established and many men actively sought wives.

Cora Lee had spent her entire life residing in a busy city. Her family had never even owned a horse, or a dog, living in an apartment above her father's shoe store. Oh, they'd been happy, the three of them. Her father had provided well for his family by making and repairing shoes, and her mother had created a wonderful, loving home for them all to enjoy.

Now her parents were gone, and Cora Lee had been left without many options for her future.

The closer she got to Holiday, the more she questioned if she'd chosen the right path. What if her intended was a horrible man, one who'd written lies to her? She'd heard about mail-order brides being deceived. There hadn't been time to exchange photographs with Jude, even if she'd had a recent one to send, which she did not.

No, the last photo that had been taken of her was carefully packed in her trunks with other keepsakes that would remind her of her parents and her heritage.

"I shall greatly look forward to our arrival in Holiday, if for no other reason than to conclude our time being tossed about on a rocking, rumbling train," Anne said as they finished in the lavatory and returned to their seats. The porter had folded up the berths, pushed aside the curtains, and made the area ready for the day.

Cora Lee nodded. "It will be nice to have this long journey behind us." She stowed her satchel beneath the seat, pinned on her hat, and settled back as the train continued chugging down the tracks.

Anne and Cora Lee purchased breakfast when the train stopped at a small town just across the Idaho border in Oregon. A farmer and his wife boarded, selling fresh milk, hot doughnuts, and boiled eggs. The two women gladly parted with a few coins for the food and enjoyed every bite as the train pulled away from the station.

Two hours later, the porter walked through the passenger car. "Baker City, folks. Baker City coming right up."

"Pardon me, sir," Anne said, smiling up at the man. "Might you be able to confirm the travel arrangements for the remainder of our journey?" She handed him her ticket.

"Yes, ma'am," he said with a friendly smile. "You'll switch trains in Baker City. The Holiday Express line will take you right into Holiday. You can't miss it. That train is a beaut, shiny like a new penny." He tipped his cap to them, returned the ticket to Anne, and continued on his way through the car and on to the next one.

"I wish we had time to explore Baker City,"

Anne said, looking out the window as the train rolled past a sea of cattle. Cowboys rode along a fence, and one of them lifted his hat, offering a jaunty wave.

"I wonder if all the men here are like that," Cora Lee asked as she gazed out the window, fighting down the urge to return the welcoming greeting.

She'd expected the landscape to be different, but nothing had prepared her for the rolling hills covered in what she'd learned was called sagebrush. It seemed almost barren, desolate, to her, although not quite as lonesome as the prairies they'd traveled across. Would Holiday be surrounded by scrubby brush, dirt, and not much else? She hoped not.

Although it was just the first day of November, she'd expected to see snow on the ground, but it appeared none had yet fallen. That, at least, made traveling easier for everyone.

She and Anne were both watching out the window as the train rolled into the station at Baker City. True to what they'd heard about the mining town, it was bustling with activity.

"Welcome to Baker City," the porter said as he took a position at the steps leading out of the car to help the women as they departed the train.

"Perhaps another time, we can travel back here to investigate what appears to be a thriving town," Anne said as they made their way over to where a train, as shiny and new as the porter said, was loading passengers. It didn't hold any sleeping cars, but the passenger car they stepped into was nicely appointed, with upholstered seats all facing forward.

"How lovely," Anne said, smoothing her gloved hand over the back of a seat. "Would you like to sit by the window or the aisle?"

"The aisle's fine with me," Cora Lee said, settling beside her friend. They slid their satchels beneath the seats, sank back against the soft cushions, and anxiously awaited the beginning of the last leg of their journey. Cora Lee took in the mahogany paneling, the stained glass framing the windows, the extraordinary details of the passenger car that made her feel like she'd entered a luxurious world she'd only dreamed of one day experiencing.

They didn't have long to wait before the train began to move and chugged away from the station. From what Cora Lee could tell, they were heading due east, but she knew from Jude's letters that Holiday was located north of Baker City.

Curious, but not concerned, she and Anne stared out the window at the hills of sagebrush.

"This must seem even stranger to you than it does to me," she said to her seatmate.

Anne turned to smile at her. "Oh, I think it is probably quite different than either of us anticipated, but perhaps there is beauty to be found in the ruggedness of this place."

"It is rather rugged," Cora Lee said, patting Anne's hand as they returned to watching out the window.

"Did you notice the name painted on the engine of the train?"

"Hope." Cora Lee thought the name of the train quite fitting. Earnestly, she hoped she'd done the right thing in agreeing to come to Holiday to marry a stranger. "I can't think of a better name for the conveyance carrying us to the end of our journey. Hope is what I have for our future, and hope is what we'll have to lean on as we begin a new life in Holiday."

"Exactly. We shall cling to hope and friendship and faith." Anne playfully bumped her arm. "And perhaps our handsome husbands."

Cora Lee laughed. "I *hope* it will be so."

As the train chugged down the tracks, it changed directions, traveling north. With each passing mile, Cora Lee grew more nervous until she felt like she might explode. What if this trip had been a huge mistake? What if Jude was a horrid man? What if she spent the rest of her life in misery?

Unable to sit still, she rose from her seat.

"Where are you going?" Anne asked, glancing from the window to Cora Lee. "Is something wrong?"

"I just need to stretch my legs a bit."

Anne nodded in commiseration. "I can hardly wait to go for a stroll through Holiday. It will be nice to walk after sitting for so many days on end." The woman rose slightly and glanced toward the back of the car. "Perhaps no one would mind if you walk from one end of the car to the other a few times."

"I guess we'll find out," Cora Lee said, taking a few steps to the front of the car. She turned, then headed toward the back. She'd nearly reached the door when the train jerked, brakes squealing, and a few passengers shouted in surprise as they ground to an unexpected, bone-jarring halt.

She cast a questioning look over her shoulder toward Anne. What on earth was happening?

Chapter Two

The force of the abrupt stop tossed Cora Lee forward. She might have crashed into the door if it hadn't suddenly swung open and a man stepped inside. The momentum of being pitched about carried her into his solid form.

Hands gripped her elbows, holding her upright. She lifted her gaze to a face that was quite handsome, at least what she could see of it around the bandana that partially covered his face. She must have inadvertently tugged it down when she'd fallen against him. She couldn't see his whole face, but she caught a glimpse of a straight nose and lips that appeared positively made for kissing. The brim of his broad hat shadowed his eyes, so she couldn't discern the color, but he had long, dark lashes.

The man released his grip on her, yanked up the bandana, and pulled a gun from a holster worn at his hip.

The realization the man was an outlaw left her lightheaded. She took a staggering step backward, tripped on her skirt, and would have fallen on her backside if he hadn't reached out the hand not holding the gun and steadied her.

For the first time in her life, Cora Lee thought she might faint as the train robber released her a second time.

"Maybe you better sit down, ma'am," he said, motioning with the gun to an empty seat to her left.

Cora Lee sank onto it and hoped the desperado wouldn't shoot her since she now knew what he looked like. Everything had happened so quickly, she wasn't certain anyone else had caught a glimpse of his face. In fact, she wasn't sure how much she'd actually seen or what she'd imagined.

Confused and terrified, she mutely remained seated next to an elderly woman who held onto a worn Bible with both hands. The woman's lips moved in a silent testament that she was deep in prayer. Absently, Cora Lee hoped Anne hadn't been tossed to the floor by the unexpected stop.

"Listen up, folks," the criminal spoke with a slight southern drawl. "As long as y'all remain seated and don't cause any trouble, no one will get hurt. I'm gonna walk through this car and collect your valuables. If ya know what's good for ya, y'all will cooperate."

He turned his head toward Cora Lee and the woman beside her and gave each of them a long glance before he moved on. In truth, Cora Lee didn't own much of value. One of her most prized possessions was her mother's pendant she wore next to her heart. She also had a ring that had belonged to her grandmother carefully tucked inside her satchel, but nothing else that anyone would want. Most of the value of her belongings came from the sentiments attached to them.

Cora Lee hoped the thief wouldn't notice the satchels she and Anne had stashed beneath their seats.

She watched as the cowboy on the wrong side of the law sauntered up the aisle, holding out a cloth sack he'd taken from his pocket. He stopped next to a wealthy couple and aimed the gun at the gentleman.

"If you don't want me to shoot your pretty little wife right between the eyes, you better empty your pockets. Now."

The man hurried to do the outlaw's bidding, as did his wife. The crook didn't stop at every seat. He seemed interested only in those who appeared to be in possession of money. He paused when he got to Anne, intently studying her. To Cora Lee, it seemed like he stood there for quite a long time, but with her heart galloping in her ears and making it impossible to think straight, it could have been mere seconds. Fearful for her friend, Cora Lee started to rise, but the woman beside her pulled her back down.

"Be still," the woman hissed beneath her breath.

Cora Lee knew one misstep and they could all be in trouble, but she still wanted to run to Anne. Instead, she remained seated and watched as the criminal finally moved through the rest of the occupants of the car. When he reached the far end, he opened the door, touched the tip of his pistol to his hat, then stepped outside.

Without a moment of hesitation, Cora Lee jumped up, raced to Anne, and threw her arms around her friend. "Are you well?"

"I'm fine," Anne said, returning her hug. "What about you? That deplorable reprobate could have killed you."

"But he didn't." Cora Lee released Anne, then leaned over, watching out the window as a group of six men rode away from the train. Two of them carried what appeared to be strongboxes. She wondered if they were full of money. She'd learned, through Jude's letters, there was a mine near Holiday as well as a lumber enterprise. The boxes could have contained the payroll of either place.

The passengers began to talk amongst themselves, speculating about the identity of the gang of robbers, and if the engineer might have been injured since the train had yet to move.

Suddenly, the door to the car swung open with such force, it would have banged against the wall if the conductor hadn't grabbed onto the handle. "Was anyone injured?" he asked as he rushed inside and closed the door behind him.

"No. We're all fine," said one of the men sitting in the front. "But he took my watch and my wife's jewels."

Then the shouts began to ring out of what those who'd been robbed had lost.

"Start a list of what was stolen, and I'll be back to get it," the conductor said before hastening to the next car.

According to the watch Anne wore pinned

inside her coat, it took nearly an hour for the train to begin moving again. By the time it rolled into Holiday, Cora Lee's enthusiasm over the possibilities of a pleasant life in Eastern Oregon had waned considerably.

She and Anne stepped off the train, ready to collect their trunks and leave behind the disgruntled passengers demanding something be done to recover the possessions the outlaw had taken.

Once they'd located their trunks, Anne and Cora Lee looked around the crowd gathered on the station's platform. There were miners, businessmen, lumbermen, a few Indians, a handful of Chinese laborers, cowboys, farmers, and three women. Two of the women were dressed in such a manner that Cora Lee wondered if they might be soiled doves.

Only one family was there, with three young children in tow, collecting the older woman who had warned Cora Lee to sit still instead of causing trouble. The woman had been right to hold her back, and she appreciated the wisdom now that the ordeal was over.

"Do you suppose they'll meet us?" Anne asked, nervously smoothing a glove over her skirt. She'd removed the duster she'd worn to protect her clothes from the dust and soot on the train and tucked it inside her satchel.

Cora Lee felt a twinge of envy as she studied her elegant friend. Anne was a proper English lady, from the top of her fashionable hat to the toes of her polished shoes. And she was lovely. So lovely and kind and sweet. The man she wed would be fortunate indeed.

Afraid to categorize her own somewhat disheveled state, Cora Lee poked in a few loose hairpins. She tried to ignore the wrinkles in her clothes, as she gazed around at the men remaining on the platform while the rest boarded the train.

A man with broad shoulders and an equally broad chest noticed them and headed their way. No hat covered his head, revealing a thick thatch of wavy golden hair that glistened in the afternoon sunshine. Cora Lee knew Jude had dark hair from his letters, but she wondered if the man walking toward them was Anne's intended. He wore a suit, carried a bouquet of autumn leaves, and possessed a gentle demeanor despite his brawny size.

Cora Lee grabbed Anne's hand and gave it a squeeze. "I might be wrong, but I think your blacksmith has arrived."

Anne's gaze swiveled from observing the passengers boarding the train to the man striding toward them with purpose in each step. Her mouth formed a perfect "O" as the man reached them, gave them both a cursory glance, then held out the bouquet to Anne.

"Miss Charles?" he asked in a hesitant voice. "Miss Anne Charles?"

When Anne remained silent, gaping at the stranger, Cora Lee jabbed her elbow against Anne's side, then smiled at the man. "This is Miss Charles. I'm Miss Cora Lee Schuster. Might you be Mr. Milton?"

Shyly, he smiled, still holding out the bouquet. "That's me. Randall Milton, but my friends call me R.C. I hope you'll both consider me a friend."

"Of course, R.C. What does the C stand for?" Cora Lee asked, pleased when Anne reached out for the bouquet and held it to her chest.

"Colin, but most folks don't know that," he said, winking at Anne. "We just have one hotel here in town, and I got you a room, Miss Charles. I figured you'd want a day or two to rest before we discuss paying a visit to the preacher."

Anne seemed to finally find her tongue as she offered R.C. a grateful look. "That is appreciated, sir. Thank you for the kindness."

"Well, shoot. No need to thank me. Just want to take good care of you. After all, it wouldn't do to start off on the wrong foot with my bride-to-be." R.C. pointed to the trunks behind them. "All of those belong to you?"

"Just these three," Anne said, tapping a finger on the tops of her trunks. "The others are Cora Lee's."

R.C. glanced around. Most people had wandered off now that the train had pulled out of the station, headed toward the mine. Cora Lee had noticed someone wearing a badge climb onto the engine right before it left the station. She wondered if he would take down a report of what had transpired on the way to Holiday.

"Is someone meeting you, Miss Schuster?" R.C. asked.

"I hope so. I came here to wed Jude Coleman."

"What?" R.C.'s eyes widened in dismay and he shook his head. "Are you sure it was Jude, miss, and not Jace? Or even Grant?"

"Jude. His name was on the letters," Cora Lee

said, experiencing a sinking feeling in the pit of her stomach. What was wrong with Jude Coleman? Why did the mention of his name elicit such a strong reaction from the blacksmith?

R.C. blew out a breath. "I'd better escort both of you to the hotel, then. With Jude, you just never know what sort of …"

"Sorry I'm late!" A man called as he crossed the platform. "Welcome to Holiday, Miss Schuster."

Cora Lee felt at a loss of words as she watched a rancher approach. He doffed his hat and waved in greeting. He was tall, handsome, and old enough to be her father. As the man rushed toward them, she wanted to hide behind Anne, or maybe R.C.

R.C. moved in front of Anne, then reached out to shake the rancher's hand. "Afternoon, Grant. Come to collect Jude's bride?"

"Yep." The man shook R.C.'s hand with enthusiasm, then turned to Cora Lee. "Miss Schuster, I'm Grant Coleman, Jude's pa. I got tied up on the ranch and couldn't get away to greet you earlier. I hope you haven't been waiting long."

"No, sir. Not long." Cora Lee had no idea what was going on, or why the man she'd agreed to marry was nowhere to be found. "Where is Jude?"

"He, um … he's out gathering in some cows, but he'll be home later. You can meet him then." Grant glanced from her to the trunks then back to her. "I'll get these trunks loaded in the wagon; then we can head over to the hotel for a bite to eat. I assume you haven't had time to eat anything."

"No, we haven't," Cora Lee agreed, unable to

put her finger on what, exactly, caused her to feel as though there was an undercurrent of tension flowing around her. "The train was delayed, and we've only just arrived."

"Delayed?" Mr. Coleman asked. "What sort of delay?"

"Robbed. A gang of outlaws boarded the train and made off with valuables. They also had a couple of strongboxes." Cora Lee picked up the satchel she'd set on top of one of her trunks.

She turned back to see Grant and R.C. exchanging worried glances.

"Was anyone hurt?" Mr. Coleman inquired as he picked up a trunk and started toward the platform steps.

"No. Not that I know of, anyway. One of the degenerates boarded our car, but he didn't hurt anyone. After the robbers departed, it took the train almost an hour to continue down the tracks."

Mr. Coleman nodded, hefted her trunk into a big wagon, then walked around to the high seat. "Let me give you a hand, Miss Schuster, but before I do, perhaps you'll introduce your friend."

"Oh, Mr. Coleman, this is Anne Charles. She came to marry Mr. Milton."

"I kinda figured that," Mr. Coleman said with a teasing smile before he thumped R.C. on the back. "This one has been counting the days until Miss Charles arrived, just like we've been awaiting your arrival, Miss Schuster."

"We?" she asked, uncertain who else resided at the ranch. Jude had mentioned the hands that worked there, and his father, but no one else.

"Well, there's me and Jude and my other son, Jace, and my sister, Mae. She'll be a good chaperone for you until you and Jude work out the particulars of when you want to wed."

Relief swept over her, pleased to discover there would be another female at the ranch. She wondered why Jude hadn't mentioned his aunt or his brother in his letters. Come to think of it, he'd mostly described the ranch, the town and where it was located, and the land around it.

Cora Lee watched as R.C. swung Anne into his wagon after he loaded the last trunk. Her friend sucked in a surprised gasp, but she could tell by the look on Anne's face she was pleased.

Full of questions she wasn't really sure she wanted to be answered, Cora Lee took the hand Mr. Coleman held out to her and climbed onto the wagon. He followed R.C. down the main street of town, stopping outside a three-story hotel with a broad porch out front and balconies on the second and third floors. In fact, it looked so new, Cora Lee wondered if touching it would leave a wet spot of paint on the fingers of her glove. Gilded letters on the big window beside the entry door proclaimed it the Holiday Hotel and Restaurant.

"This appears quite nice," Anne said as R.C. walked with her up the porch steps.

Cora Lee accepted the hand Grant offered to her and climbed down, joining her friend in studying the outside of the tidy-appearing building.

"We're all proud of the hotel. It just opened in September. We've sure been needing a place for folks to stay," Grant said, pulling open the door and motioning for Cora Lee and Anne to precede him and R.C. inside. "We had a small hotel that opened, two years ago, wasn't it?"

"Yep. Two years ago, right after the Broken Nugget Saloon closed down," R.C. said.

"Anyway, the hotel burned to the ground in March. Folks who owned it decided to move on to greener pastures. We're mighty happy to have Mr. and Mrs. Piedmont here." Grant removed the hat he wore and waved to a middle-aged couple standing behind a shiny mahogany counter where guests could check in. To the right, stairs spiraled upward. To the left of the desk, a door opened into what appeared to be a nicely appointed dining room.

"This way," Mr. Coleman said, guiding Cora Lee and Anne into the dining area. R.C. stopped to say something to the couple at the front desk, then caught up with them.

Soon, they were seated at a table for four. Anne made sure she sat beside Cora Lee, causing her to fight back giggles at the frustrated look on R.C.'s face. He most likely wanted time alone to get to know Anne instead of sharing her with Cora Lee and Mr. Coleman.

After placing orders for their food, Cora Lee turned to Mr. Coleman. "Jude mentioned in his letters the town has been here for six years. Is that right?"

R.C. snorted. "It wasn't exactly a town the first few years. More like a rowdy mining camp. Things started to change when a few businesses arrived and banded together to hire a marshal. That's when Holiday began to be a little more civilized."

"Well, it's shaping up to be a nice town now," Mr. Coleman said, giving R.C. a pointed look. "And I predict it will continue to grow as more families settle here."

"I agree," R.C. said, giving Anne a long glance. "Families are important."

"That they are," Mr. Coleman said, turning his attention back to Cora Lee.

Throughout the meal, she and Anne answered questions about where they had grown up, and they asked more questions about Holiday. As soon as they finished eating, the men escorted them back to the hotel lobby, which, Cora Lee noted, seemed quite lovely for such a primitive town. From the flocked wallpaper to the sparkling chandeliers and overstuffed furnishings, it looked as nice as anything one might find in a bustling city.

Anne gave her a hug, and the enormity of what they were both about to embark on hit her. She clung to her friend, whispering, "Be well, be safe, and be happy," in her ear before she pulled away, blinking to chase the moisture from her eyes.

"I hope to see you again soon, Cora Lee." Anne sniffled into a scented hankie she pulled from her sleeve.

"I'm sure we'll see each other. There is a church, isn't there?" Cora Lee asked, glancing at Mr. Coleman.

"Yes. Of course. Services are at ten every Sunday morning." Mr. Coleman looked to Anne. "And you are welcome to visit the ranch anytime, my dear. We'd love to have you."

Anne appeared pleased by the invitation.

"Thank you. I would like to see a western ranch."

"Then we'll make sure you do," R.C. said, placing a hand to Anne's elbow. "Let's get you settled and allow Grant to escort Cora Lee home before it grows dark."

Anne nodded, though she looked like she might cry. Cora Lee smiled once at her friend, then allowed Mr. Coleman to guide her outside and help her into the wagon.

"Do you need anything from the mercantile?" he asked as he swung the team around in a wide arc and they rolled down the relatively quiet street.

"No, I don't believe I do, sir." Cora Lee glanced at the various buildings as they drove past them. She saw the mercantile, an assayer's office, a saloon, the marshal's office and jail, and a bank before they reached the edge of town.

Mr. Coleman cleared his throat and glanced down at her with a fatherly smile. "You're welcome to call me Grant or Pops, if you like."

She nodded. "Thank you, sir."

He chuckled. "Well, I think my son is in for a grand surprise when he claps eyes on you, Miss Cora Lee Schuster. I don't think he had any idea you'd be so pretty."

Heat filled her cheeks and she ducked her head, surprised by the compliment. Cora Lee had never thought she was pretty, or anything beyond ordinary. But perhaps in a place where respectable women were few and far between, she might have her chance to shine.

It took almost half an hour to reach the ranch, although she suspected the sedate pace of the team made the trip take far longer than normal. If she didn't know better, she would have thought Grant was hesitant to take her to his home.

"Tell me about the Elk Creek Ranch," she said as they rolled along in silence.

Grant brightened. "Well, there's a topic I do so enjoy." He grinned at her. "I moved out here when my boys were both young. Their mother passed away when they were just little sprouts, and I needed a fresh start. Long before anyone struck gold, I claimed a section of land, put in fences, and started breeding Angus cattle I had shipped in from Scotland from some of my grandmother's relatives. Wait until you see them! And taste them. Mmm, mmm! The beef is so tender and full of flavor. Anyhow, once the boys were old enough, they each claimed a section of land adjoining mine. Then I started buying some of the land around us as we had funds available. We now have a sizeable ranch and a good herd of cattle to run on it."

Cora Lee merely nodded as the wagon rounded a bend and there before her was a one-story house, painted white with dark green shutters and trim. A broad porch stretched across the front of the house, and a fence surrounded the yard.

"My sister, Mae, insisted on the fence. We had a few animals get out and they ate her prized rose bush before we could get them shooed out of the yard." Grant chuckled. "That won't happen again. Mae said she'd shoot the first four-legged beast who made it past the gate."

Cora Lee hoped Mae would like her. Perhaps she could teach her about being a woman of the

West. It seemed to her she'd need all the help she could get settling into this strange land.

The front door swung open as Grant helped Cora Lee off the wagon. A woman with white hair piled on her head bustled across the porch, wiping her hands on a blue calico apron.

"Hello!" Mae called, her round face wreathed with a cheerful smile.

Cora Lee could easily envision her as the wife of Santa Claus in a children's Christmas tale. She looked exactly like a picture postcard she'd once seen of Santa and Mrs. Claus. Immediately, she liked the jolly, plump woman.

"Cora Lee Schuster, this is my sister, Mae McDonald. Mae, meet the woman who came here to wed Jude." Grant made the introduction as he hauled one of Cora Lee's trunks up to the porch.

Cora Lee hurried up the steps, taken aback by the look of shock on Mae's face. Apparently, she was unaware her nephew had sent away for a mail-order bride.

"It's nice to meet you, Mrs. McDonald," Cora Lee said quietly, uncertain what to do.

"Call me Mae, honey, and give me a hug. We're all family around here." Mae opened her arms, and Cora Lee accepted the warm embrace. The scent of cinnamon and something comforting and homey clung to the woman, putting her at ease. Mae leaned back but kept her hands on Cora Lee's arms. "My lands! Aren't you pretty? I had no idea Jude was planning to wed, but he sure is getting a lovely bride."

A blush pinked her cheeks as Cora Lee smiled

at Mae. "Thank you."

"No thanks necessary for telling the plain ol' truth. Now come on, honey, let's get you inside and settled. We'll put you in the bedroom right next to mine. I bet you'd like a hot bath, and maybe a nice cup of tea." Mae led her inside the house, and soon Cora Lee had bathed, washed her hair, and been encouraged to take a nap.

Sleep had overtaken her before her head fully settled on the pillow. She awakened to the sound of voices, a door slamming, and the clank of dishes in the kitchen.

Not wanting to miss her first meal in her new home, she quickly donned a gray and blue plaid wool gown, one of her favorite dresses. She brushed the tangles from her hair that had been slightly damp when she'd fallen exhausted on the bed. With deft fingers, she braided it, then pinned the braid on top of her head like a crown. After pulling a few strands loose to fall around her face, she pinched her cheeks, made a silly face in the mirror above the washstand, and hastened out of the room.

Mae had given her a brief tour of the house earlier. There was a large front room with a beautiful rock fireplace. Behind it was the kitchen with a big table that could easily seat ten people comfortably. To the right of the two main rooms were three bedrooms, including hers and Mae's. To the left were three more rooms, occupied by Grant and his sons.

Cora Lee stopped before moving from the hallway into the front room. She drew in a deep breath, released it slowly, then straightened her spine. With an upward tilt to her chin, she pretended she was Anne and walked into the room with all the grace she could muster. Other than a cheery fire crackling in the fireplace, the room was empty. She advanced into the kitchen to find Mae sweeping up the remnants of a broken plate and Grant red-faced. He appeared to be either angry or suffering from a bad case of indigestion.

"Well, look at you," Mae said, smiling brightly at Cora Lee. "Don't you look like a picture! Dinner is ready, and we might as well eat. Looks like it will just be the three of us." She motioned to the table that was set for four.

Confused, Cora Lee turned to Grant. "Will Jude not be here this evening?"

"No. He had to leave unexpectedly. There will be plenty of time to meet him tomorrow." Grant forced a smile and held out a hand. "Please, have a seat. I'm sure you're still worn out from your travels, but Mae is the best cook in these parts. A good meal will go a long way in making you feel better. That and a good night's sleep can cure most of what ails anyone."

Cora Lee felt fine, except for the rock of trepidation that had settled in her midsection. Something about the whole situation put her on edge. Impossible to define what it was that felt off, all she knew was that something was going on with the Coleman family, and she intended to discover what it was. She had a terrible feeling it had something to do with Jude.

She couldn't help but feel slighted that he'd sent his father to meet her in town instead of coming himself. He hadn't been at the ranch house when she'd arrived and had left again while she'd napped.

Why would a man so interested in and so intent on taking a bride not even bother to greet her when she'd traveled all the way across the country to be his wife?

None of it made sense to her, but, as Grant suggested, perhaps she just needed a filling meal and a good night's sleep. The morning might bring a new perspective, one that left her feeling less unsettled and more satisfied with the upheaval in her life.

Grant pulled out a chair for her, then one for Mae, before he took a seat at the head of the table. Out of habit, Cora Lee bowed her head and waited. Grant cleared his throat and asked a blessing on the meal and offered a few words of thanks for Cora Lee's safe arrival.

His amen had barely been uttered when the back door opened, ushering in a draft of cold air along with a man carrying an armload of wood.

"Hope I'm not too late for dinner," a deep, resonant voice spoke from behind the stack of wood in his arms.

"You're just in time, Jace," Mae said, turning in her chair. "Your father just finished saying grace."

"Well, if he wasn't too long-winded, then the food is still hot," the voice said in a tone that sounded jovial.

Wood clattered into the large box near the cook stove; then the man shrugged out of his coat, removed his hat, and unwound a scarf from around his neck, hanging them on hooks by the door. However, his back was to her the whole time, so she couldn't see much, other than he was tall with wide shoulders and a trim waist, or so it appeared by the overalls he wore with a blue woolen shirt. His hair was dark brown and cut short, but his posture appeared confident as he washed at the sink.

Her eyebrows raised of their own volition when he bent over and scrubbed his face. The view afforded to her by her position facing the sink made her think he had quite an appealing physique.

He straightened, wiped his hands and face on a towel, then turned around with a cocky grin. "I'm starving and ..."

His smile drooped. "I didn't know we had company. I would have shown better manners."

The man walked over to the table and stood behind the chair across from hers. "I'm Jace Coleman."

Recognition set in, and Cora Lee wondered if Jace's family knew he'd spent the day robbing the very train she'd arrived on just a few hours ago.

Chapter Three

Jace Coleman wanted a warm meal, a hot bath, and a comfortable bed. It didn't seem like too much to ask. Not after the trying day he'd endured.

He could smell Aunt Mae's roasting beef all the way out to the barn as he brushed down his horse, then made sure Jericho had plenty of feed and water. He visited with a few of the cowboys who worked on the ranch as they headed to the bunkhouse for the evening meal, then made his way to the house. He stopped and loaded his arms with wood, knowing it would save Aunt Mae a little work. But when he turned around from washing up at the sink, expecting to see his father, aunt, and possibly his annoying brother at the table, he felt like he'd been kicked in the stomach by one of the mules they used up at the mine.

A young woman sat at the table in Jude's chair, gaping at him with wide eyes, as though she'd seen a ghost. He had no idea who she was or where she'd come from, but she was a beauty. Hair the color of ripened wheat encircled her head like a crown. Eyes a similar hue to the berries that grew wild up in the hills in the summer were fringed with thick lashes. Pink lips that turned up slightly at the corners, like she was perpetually amused, made him curious if they'd taste as sweet as he imagined.

She wasn't a delicate-looking girl, the kind with a tendency to swoon. No, this female struck him as capable and determined with a helping measure of pluck in spite of her attractive appearance.

He felt his smile begin to fade when she scowled at him. "I didn't know we had company. I would have shown better manners."

Jace walked over to the table and stood behind the chair across from her, uncertain what to do to put her at ease. He thought it might be best to just take a seat and act like everything was fine, when clearly it wasn't, if the wild look in her eyes was any indication. "I'm Jace Coleman."

Slowly, she rose to her feet. "You!" she said, pointing a finger at him as though they'd previously met.

Baffled, Jace looked from his father to his aunt, then back to the stranger who was taller than he expected. Everything about the woman seemed to throw him off-kilter.

"What's wrong, Cora Lee?" Mae asked, placing a gentle hand on their guest's arm.

"He's one of the men who robbed the train!" the woman said, taking a step back from the table; as if she expected him to vault over it and attack her. "He's one of the outlaws!"

Mae grinned while his father tried to hide a bark of laughter behind a cough, but ended up guffawing loudly. The woman glowered at all three of them like they'd lost their minds.

Jace sighed and stepped around the table. "Look, Miss ... Cora Lee, was it?" he asked, glancing at his aunt. She nodded her head. "Miss Cora Lee, there is no way on this earth I participated in the train robbery today because I was the one driving it."

She stared at him for a full minute before she finally relaxed her tense posture. "Explain, please?"

He nodded and pulled out a chair for her. She slid onto the sea but perched on the edge as though she considered running away. Jace walked back around the table, and it was then his aunt noticed the sorry state of his attire.

"Jace Coleman! Not another pair of ruined britches." Mae threw her hands up in the air. "Just look at them!"

Jace glanced down at the tears, the smears of grease across the thighs, and mud caked from his knees to the hem. "Sorry, Auntie, it couldn't be helped."

"Was the train really robbed today?" Mae asked, handing Jace a platter of roasted beef so tender, it fell apart at the touch of his fork. He slid a generous helping onto his plate and passed the platter to his father.

"It was, Aunt Mae. We'd made the turn at the junction heading up to Cornucopia, maybe a mile past there, when I noticed something on the tracks. I had the shacks dancing before we got the train stopped, and by then we'd plowed right into a mess someone, probably the train robbers, had dragged across the tracks. There were fallen trees and piles of rocks. It took us most of an hour to get it all cleared out of the way. One tree was wedged into the cowcatcher and stuck beneath the engine. What a mess. While we were dealing with it, the Davis Gang robbed the train and took the mine payroll."

"I knew that's what they had," the woman said, surprising them with her proclamation. She glanced from him to his father. "I saw two of them carrying strongboxes as they rode away."

"Well, why in the world would you think my nephew was one of the robbers?" Mae asked as she handed Jace a bowl of creamy mashed potatoes.

"I was walking down the train aisle when the train came to an abrupt stop. It tossed me forward, right into one of the outlaws as he boarded our car. When I fell against him, the bandana covering his face dipped down revealing a portion of his face. I was so certain it was you, but I didn't actually see his entire face, or his eyes, or his chin."

"So, you saw a man about my age and size?" Jace asked, wondering if this woman was as smart as she looked. He was beginning to have his doubts. "And you naturally assumed I was the train robber?"

"No. Yes. I … um … Well, it was just … There was something about his face that held a resemblance to you."

"You don't say," Jace said, giving his father a pointed look. For the past year, he'd suspicioned his brother had ventured onto the wrong side of the law.

Until he had irrefutable evidence, his father refused to believe one of his sons could turn into a wanted outlaw and ride with a notorious gang. "Did you get a look at any of the other robbers?"

The woman shook her head. "No, I did not, other than from a distance as they rode away. They all had brown horses. Does that help?"

Grant chuckled. "That describes about eighty percent of the horses in a hundred-mile radius."

"Oh," the woman said, taking a dainty bite from the biscuit she'd buttered. "This is delicious. Thank you, Mae."

His aunt beamed at the woman then returned to eating her meal.

Jace took a few bites as he glanced across the table. "Tell me again who you are, Miss Cora Lee. Why are you here?" Surely, he'd missed some pertinent bit of information his family had shared. Had his father or Aunt Mae mentioned a guest? Not that he could recall. Then again, he'd been so busy working, they could have told him the president was coming to visit, and he might not have noticed.

"This is Cora Lee Schuster, mail-order bride from Cincinnati. She came to marry Jude."

The bite of potatoes Jace had just swallowed lodged like a lead lump in his throat, refusing to budge. He started coughing, whacking his chest with his fist while his eyes burned. Aunt Mae handed him a glass of water which he glugged down, then coughed some more.

When he could finally speak, he glowered at his father. "She's what?" he asked, fully aware his question came out more like a deafening roar.

Miss Cora Lee winced at the sound, and he did his best to calm down before he spoke again. "Jude sent for her?"

His father shot him a quelling look, then purposely changed the subject. "Was there any damage to the train?"

"No. A few scratches to the paint, but they'll take care of that at the yard tonight." Jace glanced at the woman across from him. If she really and truly intended to marry his wayward brother, he wished her all the luck in the world, because she was going to need it. She seemed sweet enough, and even reasonable for the most part, once she got past accusing him of being an outlaw. He couldn't help but ponder if she *had* seen Jude on the train.

Nothing his brother did would surprise him. Nothing at all. But he was flabbergasted to discover Jude's bride-to-be seated at the dinner table.

"Do you really drive the train?" Cora Lee asked after silence settled over the table once again.

Jace nodded and wiped his mouth on a napkin. "I do. I'm an engineer."

"Aren't they usually older?" Cora Lee gave him a studying look before dropping her gaze to her plate.

Jace grinned. "Usually, but I've known since the first time I set foot on a train I wanted to be the one to guide it down the track, so I did what I had to in order to get the job."

"And what did you do?" she asked, leaning slightly forward, as though she was interested in hearing more.

"Well, I started out working as a telegrapher at

a station house; then I got a job as a switchman. They are responsible for assembling trains and switching cars in a rail yard. Anyone who works that job for very long usually ends up missing fingers at best or deceased at worst. After that position, I spent a few months as a baggageman, and then I worked as a brakeman. Sometimes they're called shacks or brakies."

"And what does a brakeman do?" Cora Lee asked, setting her fork on her plate, awaiting his answer. Jace decided she either had an inquisitive mind, or was just good at pretending to be interested, but for what purpose he had no idea.

"A brakeman rides on top of the train. When the engineer needs to apply the hand brakes, the brakeman turns a wheel located on the roof of the car to make it stop. Generally, two brakies are on duty, one at the front and one at the back. When it's time to stop, the brakemen turn those wheels and hop from one car to the next until they meet in the middle. It takes practice to do it just right and keep the train from breaking apart or derailing or running away. There is nothing like the view on a clear summer evening from the top of the train, but brakies are also stuck out there when it's so cold your nose feels frozen and the tops of the cars are coated in slick ice."

"Oh, my," Cora Lee said, eyes widened. "It sounds dangerous."

Jace grinned again. "It can be, but then again, all jobs can be dangerous."

"How did you become an engineer?" she asked.

"After I worked my way up from brakeman to

fireman, I was promoted to engineer a year ago in June. Then, a few months ago, the Holiday Express line opened, and I was happy to return to the area to work."

"The Holiday Express line is the one we rode on today?"

"That's right," Jace said, forking a bite of his meat.

"And it goes to the mine?" the woman asked.

"Sure does," Grant answered. "That mine is one of the top producing gold mines in the whole state right now. Not only that, but the lumber mill is freighting lumber out, too. And we just sent several carloads of cattle to market."

Cora Lee's eyes brightened. "Oh, that's right. You raise beef cattle." She glanced down at her plate. "And you raised this?"

"Sure did. It's some of the best beef you'll find in the West," Grant said with pride.

Jace wanted to roll his eyes, but he instead looked at his aunt and winked. Aunt Mae knew how proud Grant Coleman was of his prized Angus cattle. If Jude ever caused any harm to the bovines at Elk Creek, he'd better be ready to run. Only then would their father toss him out on his ear like he so thoroughly deserved.

For the life of him, Jace couldn't fathom what had gotten into Jude. They used to be best friends and had dived into any number of boyish pranks and escapades together. Then Jude had started running with some fellows Jace didn't like or trust. From there, things had rapidly declined.

As he watched Cora Lee Schuster eat her meal

with impeccable manners, he couldn't help but wonder what had possessed his brother to send for a bride.

Part of the reason Jace had wanted to be an engineer was the freedom that came with the job. He'd loved seeing the country from the view offered from the engine of a fast-moving train chugging down the tracks. He'd traveled all over the West and even worked for a few months in the Nebraska and Kansas areas.

When he found out about Holiday putting in a line to run up to the mine and out to the lumber mill, he couldn't wait to apply.

Although he'd enjoyed seeing the country, he had missed being in Holiday with his family. Now, he was home almost every night and was available on his days off to help around the ranch. His dad had things well in hand, but Jace loved riding Jericho and working the cattle almost as much as he loved being an engineer.

Even though he was far from being ready to settle down or even contemplate marriage, he was far more apt to do so than his brother. Jude was irresponsible, immature, and much more likely to take up with a girl from the Ruby Palace than a respectable woman like Cora Lee.

Jace felt a pang of sorrow for her if she truly did intend to wed his brother. He had no doubt Jude would make her life one of misery.

For her sake, he hoped there was some misunderstanding and she could return to where she came from before Jude did something they'd both regret.

Chapter Four

On silent feet, Jace moved across the kitchen. A lamp on the table cast an amber glow around the room, illuminating his father as he snuck a piece of apple pie from beneath the towel where Mae had left it on the counter after supper.

"I thought I'd be able to catch you in here." Jace spoke quietly as he stepped near his dad.

Grant spun around so fast, the slice of apple pie he'd just set on his plate slid to the edge and would have plopped to the floor if Jace hadn't caught it. He nudged it back on the plate, licked the juice from his finger, then helped himself to a slice while his father glowered at him.

He filled two glasses with milk and set them on the table, then carried over his dish of pie before taking a seat next to his dad.

"What are you doing sneaking around at night?" Grant asked, waving his fork at him. "You could cause a body to have a fit of apoplexy or their heart to plumb stop with such tomfoolery."

"I wasn't the one digging into Aunt Mae's pie." Jace smirked at his dad. "Besides, we all know you can't help yourself when it comes to apple pie or chocolate cake. As quick as you think everyone is asleep, you sneak into the kitchen and steal a piece or three."

"I've never eaten three pieces," Grant blustered, then lowered his voice. "But you did catch me. Mae probably knew I'd get up to snitch a slice, which is why she made an extra pie in the first place. What are you doing up? And don't tell me it was a craving for pie."

"It is good pie, Pops." Jace licked the juice from his fork. "As for why I'm up, I want to hear the truth about why that poor girl is here, thinking Jude will marry her."

Grant's shoulders sagged and he sighed before he lifted his gaze to Jace's. "You know how your brother has been the last … well, for a while. I just thought if he had a good woman in his life, he'd change his ways and settle down, and go back to being a respectable person instead of a …"

Jace knew his father couldn't bear to admit that Jude was most likely a thief among his many other transgressions. Although Jace could envision Jude pulling a cruel prank on Cora Lee, he was certain his brother would never seek a decent woman to wed.

"I know for a fact Jude wasn't the one who wrote to Miss Schuster. He can barely sit still long enough to write a complete sentence, let alone the number of paragraphs it takes to compose a letter." Jace held his father's gaze and saw the guilt in his eyes. "You did it! You wrote the letters, didn't you?"

"Well, about that ..." Grant appeared sheepish as he pushed what remained of his pie around on his plate. "I saw no way to convince Jude to write for a bride, so I did it. I contacted a matchmaker I heard of who came highly recommended. She lives over in Grass Valley and is married to that fellow I sold a bull to last year. Do you recall Mr. Thompson? His wife is a well-to-do society gal and has run her own matchmaking business for years. She made the arrangements with Cora Lee. When it was suggested that Jude correspond with her, I couldn't very well send that sweet little gal any letter your brother might compose."

"Have you gone loco?" Jace asked, glaring at his father. "Jude will chew her up and spit her out, and then stomp all over her. That's likely in the first five minutes after he meets her."

Grant sighed again, then rubbed a hand over his head in frustration. Jace noticed his father's dark hair was turning gray at the temples, and the lines around his eyes had deepened. When had that happened? When had his father gone from being a strapping young man to looking older? He had no idea since he'd not paid close enough attention to notice it until this very moment.

But he was paying attention now and wanted to know, exactly, what his father planned to do about the innocent woman asleep in the room next to Aunt Mae's bedroom.

"What did Jude say when you told him his bride was arriving today?" Jace asked, aware Jude had been home that morning because they'd all eaten breakfast together.

"Jude expressed several opinions, none of which I will repeat. That boy is lucky God doesn't send a lightning bolt down to strike him mute after the blasphemous, horrible things he shouted. Thank goodness we were outside where Mae couldn't hear." Grant poked at his pie, then looked at Jace. "I tried to explain that I'd sent for a bride on his behalf and she was arriving today. All he needed to do was go into Holiday and meet the train."

"And he refused."

Grant nodded. "Refused to go. Refused his bride. Refused to be reasonable. He told me if I wanted a bride at the house so badly, I could marry her."

Jace tried to picture Cora Lee married to his father. Since he assumed she was close to his age, the idea left him greatly disturbed. Not only that, but the thought of her marrying his rotten brother made his stomach churn. He pushed what was left of his pie away and drained his glass of milk in a few gulps.

He studied his father a moment. Grant Coleman might be nearly fifty, but he was a handsome man without an ounce of fat on him, due to all the hard work he did on the ranch. If Jace wanted to admit it, he and his brother both looked like their dad. So much so, there was no mistaking the fact they were all part of the Coleman family.

"Would you, Pops? Marry her, I mean."

Grant looked appalled before shaking his head. "Absolutely not! She's a year younger than you and not … I would never …" He looked as though he wanted to pound something, but instead leaned back in his chair, fork clenched in his fist as he glowered at Jace. "I told you before, after your mother, I won't ever wed again. Not ever."

"Well, you've kept to that for eighteen years, Pops. I believe you. But what do you propose to do with Miss Schuster? Does she have a family she can return to in Cincinnati? Any friends who would take her in? I can't understand why a girl that pretty isn't already married."

"No. From her letters, she mentioned her parents had both passed. She was left without any resources, which is why she agreed to become a mail-order bride. And I agree, she is pretty. It seems the men of Cincinnati must be blind or stupid to have let her get away." Grant tossed Jace a hopeful glance. "Perhaps if Jude would just meet her, see she's a pretty girl and so sweet, he'd take an interest in her."

"Pops, you know as well as I do if Jude takes an interest in her without putting a ring on her finger first, it won't end well. I have a feeling my dear brother would treat her like he does the girls at the Ruby Palace."

Grant scowled. "Did Lucy Jamieson recover?"

Jace nodded. "Last I heard, she took the money you gave her, bought herself a train ticket, and disappeared."

"Can't blame her. Not after what Jude did."

Jace recalled how his brother, in a drunken stupor, had beaten one of the harlots at the Ruby Palace until two customers, hearing the girl's screams, had burst into the room and dragged him to the jail where he'd spent the night. Upon hearing what happened, Grant had gone into town, visited Lucy at the doctor's office, and left money to pay the bill, as well as give her a fresh start if she wanted it. Apparently, Lucy had wanted to get away as quickly as possible since she'd left that very day.

Or perhaps she was just terrified Jude would return and finish what he started.

"Do you honestly think that Jude will treat Miss Schuster better than he does any other woman?" Jace questioned.

His father's shoulders slumped even further. "I reckon not, Jace, but I can hope. And my dearest hope is that your brother will see the direction he's headed will only end badly. He has to change his ways before it's too late."

"I know you want him to change, Pops, but before that can happen, Jude has to want it too. Where do you suppose he is tonight? And who do you think robbed the train today?"

The shocked expression on Grant's face made it clear Jace had caught him off guard. "Surely you don't think your brother robbed the train, the very one you engineer?"

Jace raised an eyebrow. "It would be just like him to do it, then crow to his cronies how much smarter he is than me."

His father opened his mouth to argue, then snapped it shut, unable to refute the truth. "It's possible, but I just can't make myself believe one of my boys, one of my beloved sons, could stray so far from how he was raised."

"I know, Pops, but before you shove Miss Schuster at Jude, you might want to think about what it would be like for her to be married to him. He spends more time at the Ruby Palace than he does at home, at least when he's not off with his so-called friends. You think he's ready to change that? What would you do if you saw her at church one Sunday with a black eye or a bruised face, or limping because Jude had kicked her a few times?"

His father's tanned face turned pale. "I ... I ... it's not something I considered or want to think about."

"Well, you'd better get to thinking on it, Pops! I'm telling you, if you try to force them into marrying, the future for Miss Schuster will be miserable." Jace hated to be the one to toss a dose of reality into his father's far-fetched plans, but the man was attempting to orchestrate people's lives, and one of them had no idea at all what she was about to get herself into with Jude.

Jace scraped what was left of his pie into the bucket beneath the sink, then rinsed off the plate and fork and left them sitting in the sink. He turned back and stared at his father. The man looked as careworn as he'd ever seen him.

"I'm sorry, Pops, but I think you really should consider the possible outcomes before this thing goes any further."

Solemn, his father eventually nodded. "I'll think about what you said, son. Good night."

"Night, Pops."

Jace pushed away from the sink and started for his room. As he passed the table, his father reached out and grabbed his arm, pulling him to a stop.

"What about you?" Grant asked, his voice holding a hint of excitement as he stood. "What about you, Jace?"

Confused, Jace's brow wrinkled. "What about me? What are you talking about?"

"You could marry Cora Lee. I hate for that poor girl to think she came all this way for nothing. The two of you seemed to have gotten along well once she realized you weren't a train robber." Grant stood, placed a hand on Jace's shoulder, and gave it a gentle squeeze. "You'd make any woman a fine husband. You have a good job, and now that you're working the Holiday Express line, you're home most nights. Mae adores her already, and Cora Lee seemed to be quite interested in the ranch. It'd be perfect if you married her."

Jace stared at his father, convinced the man had lost every last lick of sense. Unable to stop himself, he laughed. "Me? Get married? No, thank you. After what my mother did to you, I have no more use for marriage than you do, Pops. Besides, I'm not ready to be tied down. I love my job and the freedom that comes with it. Why would I want to give that up to marry a woman I don't even know?"

"Get to know her. Court her." Grant gave Jace an encouraging look. "Would you at least think about it?"

"No! I'm not going to marry her or anyone, Pops. You made this mess, and you'll have to figure out a way to fix it without hurting her."

Grant rubbed his chin. "I suppose you're right. Could you at least be her friend, Jace? The only other person she knows besides us is another mail-order bride she met on the train."

Jace nodded. "That I can do." He thumped a hand on his father's shoulder. "Try to get some sleep, Pops. Morning will be here before we're ready for it."

His father smiled—a tired, defeated smile—then headed off to his room.

Jace cleaned his father's dishes, not wanting to leave more work for his aunt, then returned to bed.

For a while, he rested with his hands crossed beneath his head, staring up at the ceiling in the dark. A vision of golden hair braided into a crown, upturned lips twitching with humor, and gorgeous blue eyes sparkling with life kept him from falling asleep. He sighed and rolled onto his side, wondering what in the world they were going to do with Miss Cora Lee Schuster. One thing he knew for certain, though. Before he'd allow Jude to get his filthy hands on her, Jace would marry her himself.

And that was the last thing he wanted to do.

Chapter Five

Lazily, Cora Lee stretched in bed, enjoying the soft mattress, the fluffy pillows, and the warm bedding that smelled of sunshine and Christmas, with a hint of pine trees.

Christmas? Pine trees?

Her eyes popped open as she sat up, and she looked around an unfamiliar room. Then it all came back to her. She was in Holiday, Oregon, at Elk Creek Ranch, where she'd come to marry Jude Coleman who didn't seem particularly eager or interested in meeting her.

Her reluctant groom-to-be had run off goodness only knew where yesterday while she was napping and hadn't reappeared before she'd gone to bed. Grant Coleman had made plenty of excuses for his absent son, but Cora Lee wasn't sure she should believe them. Especially not after meeting his other son, Jace. At first, she was sure Jace had been the man who'd helped rob the train. Even though she hadn't gotten a good look at the outlaw's face, something about Jace, about the way he looked and moved, made her think they were the same man.

Of course, when Jace explained he was the train's engineer, she knew for certain he wasn't the man who'd walked through the passenger car with a gun drawn, ready to shoot anyone who didn't follow his wishes.

But because of the niggling notion in her mind that Jace seemed familiar, she couldn't let go of the idea that perhaps the thief was Jace's brother. Then again, Grant had told her Jude had been out rounding up cattle most of the day, so surely it was impossible for him to do that and rob the train too.

Unless he hadn't really been out with the cattle. Or had only pretended to be.

A dull headache began to throb behind Cora Lee's eyes. This was a fine way to start her first day in what was to be her new home. At least it would be if she married the mysterious Jude.

She flopped back on her pillows, willed herself to relax, and slowly opened her eyes. Her gaze roved around the room, taking in the beautiful light oak washstand and dresser that matched the bed where she'd slept. The pieces were hand-carved with lovely, ornate flowers etched into the wood. Something about the woodwork made her think of her parents, reminding her of how much she missed them.

Rather than dwell on her grief, she rose from the bed, rushed to dress in the chilly morning air, then took a few moments to unpack her trunks. Lovingly, she held a white woolen cape that had belonged to her mother. A design of tiny flowers and flourishes had been embroidered along the neck, down the front placket, and around the hem. Cora Lee had always called it her mother's Christmas cape. It was something her mother had only worn for special occasions, so it still looked almost like new.

Carefully, Cora Lee rewrapped it in the paper she'd secured it in when she'd packed the trunk and set it back inside where it was protected and safe.

Safe.

What an interesting word.

Cora Lee wasn't sure she'd felt safe for a long while. Not since she'd lost both of her parents. And she certainly hadn't felt safe in Holiday, not after the train was robbed.

As she brushed her long hair, braided it, then fastened it on her head, she wondered how Anne had fared last night. At least her friend had a nice room at the hotel. Cora Lee hoped it was half as nice as her room here at the ranch.

She tucked in the last hairpin, then strode over to the window, brushing aside the ruffled white curtains to look outside into the darkness that had yet to give way to dawn. From her room, she could see a few lights in the distance and wondered if it was another ranch or farm. She'd have to ask Mae about it.

Refreshed after a good night's sleep, Cora Lee felt ready to take on the day, even if she wasn't sure how things would transpire. Would Jude show his face today? Or would Grant design a dozen new excuses to explain his absence?

Cora Lee opened her bedroom door, grateful

for the warmth that greeted her when she stepped into the hall. She followed the scent of coffee through the front room and into the kitchen, where Mae was already at the stove with an apron tied around her ample waist as she placed sausages in a large skillet to fry.

"Good morning," Cora Lee said, greeting the grandmotherly woman with a smile.

"Good morning, Cora Lee." Mae offered her a welcoming smile, then turned back to the sausages. "I thought perhaps you'd sleep in today. You have to be completely worn out from your trip."

"I'm feeling ever so much better today. The room is lovely, and the bed is so comfortable. Thank you." Cora Lee looked around to see if there was anything she could do to assist Mae. When she dressed, she'd pulled on an older dress and one of the aprons she'd brought with her. "How may I help you?"

Mae gave her a studying glance, then tilted her head toward a pile of potatoes. "If you want to peel and fry half of those for breakfast, we'll cook the rest to go with a roasted chicken for lunch."

Cora Lee nodded in agreement. "Do you fry your potatoes with onion and a little bacon grease?"

Mae appeared a little startled, but then she beamed at Cora Lee. "Yes, I do. You know how to cook?"

Cora Lee nodded as she began peeling potatoes and cutting them into thin slices. "My mother taught me. She came from a long line of bakers. My family has owned the same bakery for more than a hundred years."

"Really?" Mae asked as she finished with the sausages, then washed her hands. "Where is the bakery located? Is it still in your family?"

"In Germany. My uncle and his wife took it over, last I heard." Cora Lee hadn't heard from any of her mother's relatives for a while, but she had written to let them know she was moving and where they could contact her in the future.

If things worked out, she thought she could learn to enjoy living in Holiday. Everything seemed so different here than the city. So much cleaner and quieter and more peaceful.

"Do you like to bake?" Mae asked as she made biscuits.

"I do, particularly at Christmas time. My mother and I would bake all sorts of things and make candies. We had the best time in the kitchen. On Christmas Eve, we'd deliver treats to our neighbors and friends." Cora Lee felt tears burning behind her eyes and blinked them away. This would be her first Christmas without her parents. The first Christmas away from the place she'd always considered home.

"I'd love to bake with you, Cora Lee. Perhaps we could share recipes with each other."

"Oh, that would be lovely, Mae. Thank you," Cora Lee tamped down her melancholy and smiled at the older woman. "Do you have ..."

Before she could ask her question, the back door swung open, and Jace stepped inside, carrying a milk bucket in one hand and a basket full of eggs in the other.

"Thank you, honey," Mae said, smiling at Jace

as he toed the door shut, then set the bucket of milk in the sink.

Since Cora Lee was working on one end of the sink, she scooted over when Jace washed his hands, then reached for a pitcher and a piece of thin cloth. With interest, she watched as he strained the milk into the pitcher, rinsed the cloth, and hung it to dry on the peg where he'd taken it from, then washed out the bucket.

"Good morning," he said softly, casting a quick glimpse her way.

He acted as though he were afraid she'd bolt if he looked her full in the face. To prove she was made of sterner stuff, she moved a step closer to him. "Good morning, Mr. Coleman. Your aunt and I were just talking about baking treats for Christmas."

A boyish grin lit up his handsome face. Cora Lee found herself drawn to his warm hazel eyes. How could she have mistaken this man for a robber? He seemed far too amiable and kind to ever do such a despicable thing.

"Will you bake all my favorites, Auntie Mae?" Jace questioned his aunt, although his gaze remained fastened to Cora Lee's face.

"Of course, honey, but only if you bring me the ingredients when I'm ready for them. You know the mercantile doesn't carry many of the special items we'll need."

"You make a list when you're ready to start baking, and I'll make sure you have everything you need. I'm quite partial to sweets." He winked at Cora Lee, picked up the milk bucket and the egg basket Mae had emptied, then returned outside.

"He's a good man, Cora Lee, even if he can be a bit of a rascal," Mae said as she cracked a few eggs into a bowl and began stirring in sugar. From what Cora Lee could tell, Mae was mixing up a cake.

Uncertain what to say to Mae about Jace, she remained silent as she finished peeling the potatoes. The skillet was hot, and the spoon of bacon grease she dropped in sizzled and popped as it melted. She added the potatoes and the bit of onion she'd chopped, then set a lid on the skillet while Mae poured cake batter into a pan.

"Would you like to go to church with us this morning?" Mae asked after she'd slid the cake into the oven.

Somehow, in all the excitement of arriving in Holiday and the challenges of travel, she'd lost track of the days.

"I'd forgotten today is Sunday," Cora Lee said, glancing down at her worn dress and apron. "I'd very much like to attend, but I'll need to change before we go."

Mae laughed. "We have plenty of time, honey. The menfolk will want to clean up after they finish the chores, so you'll have time to change if you wish."

Cora Lee nodded in understanding and helped set the table.

Three and a half hours later, she stood in front of the dresser mirror in her room, giving herself a critical eye. Rather than wrapping her hair in a braid like a crown, she'd fashioned it in a low knot at the back of her head to accommodate the hat she intended to wear. It had been her mother's very best hat, and one she'd always admired. Her father had purchased it as a gift for her mother for her birthday three years ago.

The dark blue wool matched Cora Lee's best coat, one her parents had given to her for Christmas last year. She'd packed it in a trunk instead of wearing it on the train, mindful of the soot that she might never get out of it, although Mae had promised she could get her traveling suit clean again.

Cora Lee had her doubts the suit would ever look the same, but she did want to put her best foot forward this morning as she met people of the community at church.

She was glad she'd taken the time to add to the hat pale blue ribbons and a silk rose in the same shade. Today, she'd chosen to wear a navy blue dress with a floral-patterned stripe in a pale shade of blue. When paired with the hat, it made quite a striking combination, or so she'd been told when she'd worn the ensemble back home.

After poking in a few extra hairpins to make sure her hair stayed in place, she pinned on the hat, picked up her coat and reticule, then made her way to the front room.

Grant sat in a heavy leather chair located closest to the fireplace with an open Bible on his lap. The sound of dishes clanking in the kitchen let her know where she could find Mae. Jace was nowhere to be seen. Perhaps he didn't plan to attend the services. Part of Cora Lee hoped that was the case. Something about him made her feel nervous and fluttery inside, and she wasn't entirely certain she liked the strange sensations his presence produced. She'd experienced it yesterday, then again this morning. All through breakfast, she battled the feeling that she'd somehow swallowed a legion of butterflies and they were all trying to wing their way to freedom.

Amused with her silly thoughts, she grinned as she set down her coat and reticule.

"Ready to go?" Grant asked, offering her a friendly smile as he closed the Bible and set it on the table by his chair.

"Yes, I believe so. Do I need to bring my Bible?"

"No. Not unless you want to. I'm just doing a little extra reading because it's my turn this week to offer the opening prayer."

Cora Lee tilted her head to one side. "Doesn't the church have a pastor?"

"We do, indeed, but he likes to ask a member of the congregation to offer the opening prayer every week. And to make it easier, he asks ahead of time. Actually, I'd probably stew a lot less about it if he just called on me during the service." Grant rose and gave Cora Lee an admiring glance. "You sure look nice today, Cora Lee. Do you sew?"

"A little. My mother was a wonder with a needle and thread. She made most of my things." Cora Lee ran a hand down the skirt of her gown, wishing her mother were still alive. She'd trade everything she owned, which had been packed into three trunks, to have her parents back again, even for just a few hours with them.

Since that was impossible, she planned to rely on sweet memories to keep them close at heart.

"Oh, what a beautiful gown," Mae said as she breezed in from the kitchen. She wore a gray dress accented with soft pink lace that brought out the rosy hue of her cheeks and the shine of her silvery-white hair.

"Thank you, Mae," Cora Lee smiled at her. "You look beautiful too."

Grant chuckled as he plucked Mae's coat from a hook by the door and held it for her. "I'm feeling fortunate to be able to escort two lovely ladies to church this morning."

He'd just reached for Cora Lee's coat when the front door swung open and Jace stepped inside, capturing her attention. She had no idea he could clean up so well.

Yesterday, he'd been dirty and tired and wearing his engineer uniform of blue overalls when she'd met him at dinner. This morning, he'd had on a flannel shirt and worn denims while he was doing the chores. Now, he appeared quite dashing in a pair of pressed trousers with a starched shirt and perfectly knotted tie beneath his heavy woolen coat. A hat like the ranch hands wore and a pair of polished boots kept him from looking too citified, though.

"It's cold out there," he said, rubbing his hands together. "I threw in some extra blankets for the ladies."

"That's thoughtful of you, honey," Mae said, reaching up to pat his cheek as she hurried out the door.

Cora Lee slipped her arms into the sleeves of her coat, then pulled a pair of gloves from the pocket and tugged them on her hands. She snatched up her reticule and trailed after Mae, not wanting to be left alone with Jace for even a moment or two.

Grant followed her outside, tugging on his coat as he went, then hurried over to offer Mae a hand as she climbed into the back seat of a black buggy with crimson wheels.

Cora Lee tried to hide her surprise at seeing the snappy conveyance. She'd fully anticipated being transported to town in the back of the big farm wagon.

"This buggy is very nice," she said as Jace helped her in. Even through her glove she felt a tingle travel up her arm when their hands connected. Unwilling to consider the reason for her reaction to the man, she took a seat next to Mae and leaned back as Grant tossed a blanket over their laps.

"Pops traded a bull for it a few years back," Jace said as he slid onto the front seat and lifted the reins in his hands.

Grant settled next to him, then looked back at Cora Lee and Mae. "One of the best trades I've made," he said with a grin. "Mae likes to ride to church in style, or when she's heading into town."

Mae shook her finger at her brother. "Now, Grant Coleman, you tell the truth. You enjoy rolling into town in this shiny buggy just as much as anyone else. In fact, the Widow Truman practically swoons every time she sees you driving it through Holiday."

Red crept up Grant's neck and stained his ears as he glowered at Mae before he shifted so he faced forward rather than looking back.

Mae chuckled and winked at Cora Lee as Jace snapped the reins and the horse pulled away from the house.

The horse, a big black gelding, kept an easy gait as they headed down the lane. Cora Lee thought he was a gorgeous animal and one that seemed well-behaved, too.

"What's his name?" she finally asked, looking to Mae.

"Who?"

Cora Lee motioned to the horse. "The fine steed pulling us to town."

Mae grinned. "Oh, that's Eb."

"Short for Ebony?" Cora Lee inquired.

Jace laughed. "No, Ebenezer."

"As in Ebenezer Scrooge? From Dickens' work?" Cora Lee couldn't believe anyone would name such a majestic animal after a tight-fisted curmudgeon.

"That's the one," Grant said, glancing back at her. "His previous owners couldn't get him to do anything they wanted and declared him to be as stubborn and set in his ways as ol' Ebenezer."

"Pops traded them an old nag for Eb. Within six months, he was like a brand-new horse," Jace said, smiling at her over his shoulder.

She couldn't help but notice the white teeth that gleamed against the tan of his face, nor the way his smile accentuated his strong chin with the slightest cleft right in the center of it. Distracted by him, by his rugged masculinity, she found herself leaning forward, drawing closer to him.

When she realized what she'd done, she settled back on the seat and primly folded her hands together, blaming the weary days of travel and upsetting circumstances of being involved in a train robbery for her odd behavior.

Mae began pointing out farms and houses as they turned onto the road that would take them into town, telling her who lived where. As they reached Holiday, Mae scowled at a two-story house painted a shocking shade of red. A gilded sign hanging out front made it known the establishment was the Ruby Palace.

Cora Lee could only assume the type of business that took place there. A man strolled out the front door, hands shoved in his pockets. When he glanced up at them, he yanked his hat down to hide his face and turned the other way, beating a hasty retreat.

Uncertain what to make of the man's behavior, she couldn't miss the condemning look on Mae's face or the hard set to Jace's jaw as she glanced at his profile. They knew the man, whoever he was. Grant had been looking across the street and seemed unaware that Jace and Mae both seemed distressed. Surely the man wasn't Jude!

Good heavens! If her intended had spent the night at such a place, she would have nothing to do with him. Nothing at all!

She had managed not to question the lack of his presence at breakfast, but now she simply wanted to know where he could possibly be. To her, it seemed as if he was hiding, perhaps hoping she'd give up and leave him in peace. If that was the case, she would leave immediately. Although she had no idea where she'd go and limited funds, she refused to stay somewhere she wasn't wanted.

Unable to contain her thoughts any longer, she looked over at Mae. "Will Jude be at church this morning?"

A snort rolled out of Jace, and Mae smacked him on the back with her reticule. He glanced at his aunt, then returned his gaze to the street. He spoke in such a quiet tone, Cora Lee was sure he didn't mean for his words to be heard, but she caught them. "Only if the pastor moves the services to the Ruby Palace."

Cora Lee straightened on the seat, sitting as upright as a stiff board. No one had said anything for sure, and she had no proof, but everything in her screamed a warning that Jude was not the best choice for a husband.

Jace had barely stopped the buggy outside the church when Cora Lee caught sight of Anne, standing by the door with R.C. Milton. The man towered over her tiny friend, but he looked thoroughly besotted. For that matter, Anne appeared rather smitten, too.

Cora Lee waved to her friend, eager to hear how she liked Holiday and the handsome R.C. Jace gave her a hand out of the buggy, and that strange tingling threaded up her arm again. She tamped down the urge to see if he held something on his palm that caused her reaction and rushed over to Anne's side.

The two women hugged, and then Cora Lee offered R.C. a smile. "Good morning, sir."

"Mornin', Miss Cora Lee. Are you enjoying your stay at the Elk Creek Ranch?" R.C. asked, keeping a hand on Anne's tiny waist.

"I've enjoyed what little I've seen of it. Admittedly, I've remained in the house and haven't yet explored." She glanced over at the Coleman family as they approached her.

Grant doffed his hat and tipped his head to Anne. "Miss Charles. Looks like Holiday is agreeing with you."

"It certainly is, Mr. Coleman. It certainly is." She looked up at R.C. with her heart in her eyes, and Cora Lee knew that her friend was already in love.

Grant made the introductions, and Cora Lee watched Jace to see how he reacted to her beautiful friend. He remained polite, yet aloof. However, with R.C. he did seem more relaxed. Cora Lee quickly surmised the two of them were good friends.

Anne took both of Cora Lee's hands in hers. "I realize it is short notice, but would you stand up with us after the service? R.C. and I want to wed right away. He's already talked to the pastor, who agreed to perform the ceremony following the church service."

"Oh, Anne! I'd be honored," Cora Lee said, hugging her friend again.

R.C. grinned at Jace. "I was hoping you'd stand up with me."

"Of course, R.C. Thank you for asking me,"

Jace said, thumping his friend on the back. "Congratulations!"

R.C. tipped his head toward Cora Lee. "You know, it's not that hard to order a bride and fall in love."

Jace glowered at him and backed away. "Don't go getting any ideas. I'm perfectly happy with my life the way it is and have no plans to change it."

Before anyone could goad him, Jace jogged up the church steps and pulled open the door, waiting as they all trooped inside.

When Cora Lee walked past him, she was almost positive she heard him draw in a deep breath, but surely it was her imagination.

Grant led the way to the third pew from the front on the left side of the pulpit. Cora Lee wasn't sure how it happened, but she ended up sitting between Jace and Anne. Her friend was so focused on the man she would soon wed, Cora Lee wasn't sure she even realized anyone else was in the church.

Under the guise of searching in her reticule for something, Cora Lee cast a quick glimpse around, taking in a good number of attendees in the congregation. Several couples made her hopeful that she would meet more women in town who might become friends.

A young man in a well-worn suit approached the pulpit. "Good morning, friends. Please open your hymnal to page eighty-seven."

Cora Lee realized there weren't enough hymnals for each person to use, so she had to share with Jace. He turned to the correct page, and she listened, surprised, when he joined in the singing with a smooth, resonating voice. Since the hymn was one she knew, she didn't need to see the words, but she focused on the hymnal instead of the man holding it. Surreptitiously, she indulged in a covert look at his face and found him watching her. Like a mischievous boy, he grinned at her, then began to sing with a little more enthusiasm.

When the last note of the hymn faded, the pastor stepped aside and Grant hurried up to the pulpit. He offered a heartfelt prayer Cora Lee found quite touching; then he returned to his seat, and the pastor began his sermon.

It amazed her that a pastor who appeared as young as the man behind the pulpit could speak with such insight and joy for God's word. His sermon left Cora Lee hungry to spend some time at home reading through the verses he referenced.

After the final hymn was sung and the pastor offered the closing prayer, he held up a hand to stop anyone from moving.

"I am delighted to announce R.C. Milton and Anne Charles have invited you all to stay to witness their nuptials. They will exchange vows in about ten minutes. If anyone needs to leave, please do so quietly. Otherwise, if you all remain in your seats, we'll have a wedding shortly."

The congregation began to buzz, and the pastor's grin widened. "For those of you who haven't yet met her, Anne Charles is seated there beside R.C. And next to her is another new arrival, Miss Cora Lee Schuster. Welcome to Holiday and our little church."

Cora Lee never liked to be the center of attention. For Anne's sake, she politely smiled and followed her friend to the front of the church, where the pastor waited to give them all instruction. Jace and Grant joined them while Mae went to the piano and began to quietly play a selection of hymns.

"May I walk you down the aisle, Miss Charles?" Grant asked.

Anne turned to him with a teary smile. "I would very much like that, Mr. Coleman. Thank you."

"If Miss Charles and Grant would like to go to the back of the church, Jace and Miss Schuster may remain up here with R.C., and we can get things started." The pastor nodded to Cora Lee. "It's nice to meet you, Miss Schuster."

"I'm happy to make your acquaintance, Pastor Ryan." Cora Lee smiled at him, glad she'd thought to ask Mae the pastor's name before they arrived at the church. It might have been nice if the woman had explained that John Ryan was not only a pastor, but also young and quite attractive. Since no one had mentioned a wife, Cora Lee assumed he was not yet married.

"Oh, I almost forgot the bouquet!" R.C. said, racing down the aisle and out the door. He was gone only a few minutes. When he returned, he handed something to Anne that Cora Lee couldn't see, then took his place beside the pastor once again.

"Are we ready?" Pastor Ryan asked.

"Yep." R.C. nodded his head, putting Cora Lee in mind of an eager puppy.

Comparing the brawny blacksmith to a puppy

made her want to laugh, so she turned her attention to the back of the church. Mae began playing a song perfect for a bride walking down the aisle.

Anne floated toward them, one hand lightly resting on Grant's arm while she held a bouquet of autumn flowers and leaves with the other. Cora Lee had no idea where R.C. had acquired the bouquet, but it was almost as beautiful as his bride.

The pale wool gown Anne wore, in a shade that reminded Cora Lee of the last fading lilacs of spring, was simple in style but elegant, with thick lace around the collar, cuffs, and along the front. A matching hat perched on her head at a sassy angle, and a smile lingered around her lips.

No wonder R.C. was already in love with her friend. Anne was breathtaking.

Through the brief ceremony, Cora Lee wondered what it would be like to be so instantly in love and to have it returned. Her glance drifted to Jace as he stood next to R.C. Thoughts of him sliding a ring on her finger made her long to feel the warmth of his hand against hers. She couldn't say what it was about Jace that drew her attention, but something definitely did.

Her interest in Jace was precisely the reason she needed to ignore him, ignore the feelings he stirred in her. She was there to marry his brother, not him. At least that was her intention if Jude ever bothered to show up, and, if in fact he had not robbed the train or spent the night frequenting the Ruby Palace.

"I now pronounce you husband and wife," Pastor Ryan said, beaming at R.C. and Anne. "You may kiss your bride."

R.C. wasted no time in pulling Anne into his arms. He gave her a heated kiss that made Cora Lee blush, Jace chuckle, and a few members of the congregation whistle.

Mae looked like she considered marching over to R.C. and smacking some sense into him with the hymnal she held in her hand. Before such action was necessary, the blacksmith raised his head, smiled at his wife, then swept her into his arms and carried her out of the church amid cheers and shouts of "congratulations!"

Cora Lee felt a hand on her elbow at the same time her skin began to tingle. She knew without looking it was Jace as he escorted her back to the pew where they'd left their coats. Not only could she feel his presence, but he had the most alluring, enchanting scent that smelled of leather and pine and something she couldn't aptly describe but enjoyed all the same.

Jace held her coat as she slipped it on while Grant helped Mae with hers. Together, the four of them made their way to the back of the church where the pastor stood at the door, shaking hands with everyone.

"It really is so nice to meet you, Miss Schuster. I'm so pleased you've decided to make Holiday your home," the pastor said, holding onto her hand a moment longer than necessary.

"Thank you, Pastor Ryan. From what I've seen so far, Holiday seems to be a nice town."

"It is." The pastor reluctantly released her fingers, then reached out to shake Jace's hand. "I'm glad to see you weren't hurt in the train robbery yesterday. I heard from the marshal no one was seriously injured, although the men guarding the payroll were knocked unconscious."

Jace nodded. "It could have been worse." He glanced at Cora Lee, then nudged her toward the door. "Much worse."

The pastor nodded before turning to greet those standing in line behind them.

Although it was sunny outside, it was so cold the breath of those visiting on the brown grass of the church lawn rose in frosty plumes like steam released from a boiling kettle.

Mae introduced Cora Lee to the women who'd gathered together to discuss their next quilting bee. Grant introduced her to the doctor, the marshal, and the stationmaster of the depot.

By then, she was thoroughly chilled and more than ready to return to the ranch. Much to her relief, Jace suggested they head home and helped her into the buggy. All the way there, her mind wandered to Anne and how happy her friend seemed. Cora Lee hoped she'd someday know love. To love and be loved. Her parents had given her such a good example of what it meant to be married to a true partner in life. Not once had she ever questioned their love and devotion to one another. It was evident in their words, their actions, even the way they looked at each other. And Cora Lee refused to settle for anything less than the devotion her parents shared.

What had she been thinking, agreeing to travel so far out West to marry a man she'd never met?

Her parents were probably rolling over in their graves, appalled at what she'd done.

When she finally met Jude, if she didn't feel he would be suitable as a spouse, she would simply leave the ranch. She'd find a job, pay the Coleman family for her train ticket and their hospitality, then move on elsewhere.

But the thought of never seeing Mae, Grant, Anne, or even Jace again made a lump settle in her throat.

Cora Lee tried to rein in her thoughts and get control of her emotions before they reached the ranch. As Jace guided the buggy to a stop outside the house, Cora Lee felt like she had come home. Shocked by how much she liked being at Elk Creek Ranch, even in so short a time, she had no idea what to do about it. If she married Jude, would they continue to live on the ranch? And if she refused to marry him, would she ever be welcome there again?

Cora Lee accepted the hand Grant held out to her as he helped her and Mae out of the buggy. The three of them went inside the house, while Jace said he'd see to the horse.

"Go change out of that dress, honey. You don't want to spill anything on it," Mae said, leading the way down the hallway to their rooms. "I'll just be a minute while I change."

Cora Lee hurried into her room and changed into a woolen dress that had been her mother's. The dark brown hue was not her favorite color, but the gown was warm and had been worn enough she didn't worry about ruining it.

She returned to the kitchen to find Mae already

there, pulling the roasting pan from the oven. The mouth-watering aroma of baked chicken had filled the house with a delicious fragrance that made them all eager to eat as soon as they walked inside.

Jace entered through the back door, carrying another load of wood that he deposited in the wood box before he disappeared down the hall on the other side of the kitchen. He returned a few minutes later, dressed in clothes that looked warm but worn.

"Everything is ready," Mae said, setting a bowl of potatoes on the table. "Jace, it would be nice if you asked the blessing."

Jace offered a prayer, then the four of them began passing around bowls and plates.

Cora Lee waited until the meal was nearly over before she looked to Grant. "Do you think Jude will return today?"

He offered her a smile, although it looked a little forced. "I'm not sure, Cora Lee, but don't you fret about Jude. He'll be here soon enough, and I'm sure he'll be so pleased to meet you. After all, he did send for you."

Jace made a noise that sounded like a growl, but when Cora Lee looked over at him, he appeared to be coughing into his napkin. She glanced at Mae and caught her glowering at Grant.

They all knew something they weren't telling her. And she intended to get to the bottom of the curious matter. In the meantime, she would enjoy getting to know the Coleman family and staying at the ranch for as long as they welcomed her.

Chapter Six

Jace stamped the snow from his boots, then pushed open the back door and stepped into the kitchen.

"I'm home!" He dumped an armful of wood into the box by the stove, brushed stray bits of wood and bark off his coat into the box, then drew in a deep breath. The aroma of roasting meat and yeasty bread mingled with cinnamon and apples, making his stomach grumble with hunger.

He turned around to find the kitchen empty except for Cora Lee. She stood at the stove, stirring something in a saucepan. The sight of her made his pulse kick into an accelerated pace. Everything about Cora Lee Schuster fascinated him, from the way she wore her glorious golden hair braided into a crown around her head to the manner in which the bow of her apron bobbed at her waist with every movement she made.

She glanced over her shoulder at him with a friendly smile. "Hi, Jace. Welcome home."

Despite the lecture he'd given himself earlier to stay away from her, Jace couldn't keep his distance. Not when he so enjoyed being near her. In the three weeks she'd been at the ranch, he'd spent quite a bit of time with her, becoming acquainted with her. He'd found her to be witty and intelligent, amusing, and fun, but also cautious and somewhat guarded.

Not that he could blame her.

Jude had made it clear he held no interest in getting married. In fact, his wayward brother had disappeared the Sunday they'd seen him coming out of the Ruby Palace on their way to church and still had yet to meet Cora Lee.

Jace had checked his brother's room after they'd returned from church that day to find Jude had returned home long enough to pack a bag. Based on what was missing from the room, he'd taken several changes of clothes, and a few guns. Jude had also raided the household money their father kept in a tin box in his desk in the front room. The hastily scrawled note his brother had left on the desk stated he refused to marry "that wench," as he referred to Cora Lee, and would be back when she was gone.

Since they preferred Cora Lee's company to Jude's, none of them were in a hurry to tell her Jude refused to marry her.

Instead, his father kept up the ruse that Jude had to make an unplanned trip and would return as soon as possible.

To her credit, Cora Lee played along with it, even though Jace was sure she had to suspect something by now.

He and his father had argued several times about telling her the truth. Jace thought it was wrong not to explain everything to her, but his father still held out a glimmer of hope that Jude would change his mind and come home to claim the bride awaiting him.

A need to protect and shelter Cora Lee made Jace clench his hands into fists and want to pummel Jude every time he thought of his brother touching the sweet woman. Jace had never experienced such a primitive urge to bash someone as he had since meeting Cora Lee. He wasn't certain if it was the woman herself who drew out such cavedweller-like tendencies, or the notion of any unsuspecting female marrying his wayward brother.

But as he looked across the kitchen at Cora Lee, he knew he'd do anything to keep her safe, especially from Jude.

He crossed the distance between them in a few long strides, then looked over her shoulder to observe what appeared to be some kind of sauce. He could see she had meat frying in a skillet of hot lard, and two pots bubbled and boiled, emitting interesting aromas.

"How are you, Cora Lee?" he asked, bending close enough to stir the tendrils of hair that curled around her ear. A shiver trailed over her, and he bit back a smile, pleased she wasn't completely immune to him or his presence. He took a breath, savoring the soft, feminine scent of her that put him in mind of autumn flowers and apple pies.

"I'm well, Jace. Did you have a good run today?" she asked as she subtly shifted to the side, moving away from him.

He took a step back and nodded. "I did have a good day. How about you?" He looked around the kitchen again. "Where's Aunt Mae?"

"Mr. Garbaldi came and got her earlier. His wife is, um ... well, their baby is on the way, and the doctor was up at the mine. It seems a few of the workers were injured this morning, and he was seeing to them."

Jace knew his aunt had helped with a few births when the doctor wasn't available. She seemed to enjoy it, and he knew her steady, calm presence was most likely a blessing to the women she assisted.

"So, you took over fixing supper?" Jace asked as he removed his coat and hat, leaving them on pegs by the door before he washed his hands at the sink.

"Yes. I hope no one minds. I enjoy cooking, and Mae has been so good to let me help since I've been here. Honestly, I feel like I don't do enough to earn my keep."

"I'm sure whatever you made will be wonderful. As to earning your keep, that is unnecessary. You know you are our guest for as long as you want to be here," Jace said, smiling at her as he dried his hands. "What can I do to help?"

"If you'd like, you could set the table. The food will be ready soon." Cora Lee took a baking pan from the oven, then poured the sauce she'd been stirring over the top.

"What's that?" he asked, unable to hide his curiosity as she set the pan aside to cool. He was sure it held a dessert. At least he hoped the apple and cinnamon aromas wafting from it meant that was what they'd enjoy after dinner.

"Apple cake. It's my grandmother's recipe."

"Is that the grandmother that had the bakery?" Jace asked, recalling her talking about her family owning a bakery in Germany in one of their conversations last week.

"That's right." Cora Lee bent over to take something else from the stove, and Jace couldn't help staring at her, admiring her womanly form. She might be more cute than beautiful, but he thought she was exceptionally attractive, and more importantly, a good person with a kind heart.

"Are we having a traditional German meal for supper?" he asked, setting forks and knives by the plates.

"We are. I hope you and your father will like it."

"You may have noticed we aren't picky eaters, Cora Lee. Besides, from what I've tasted, you are an excellent cook."

She blushed and turned back to the stove as he retrieved the milk pitcher from where they kept it in a sawdust-insulated cabinet built into the wall on the back porch. A narrow door allowed access to it from inside the house. With more than a foot of snow on the ground, the cold temperatures kept the perishable food they stored in it from spoiling. In the spring, they used ice they cut into blocks during the winter and stored in the cellar in crates packed with sawdust to keep food cold.

Jace filled three glasses with milk and carried them to the table. The door swung open and his father made his way inside, brushing snow from his shoulders.

"Mae still gone?" he asked as he removed his hat and shook off the snow outside before he closed the door.

"Yes. I hope she spends the night with the Garbaldi family instead of trying to make it back in this storm," Cora Lee said, pushing aside the curtain over the sink and staring outside into swirling snow. "Although, I suppose it isn't exactly proper for me to be here alone with you two."

Grant grinned as he hung up his coat and removed his boots. "I won't tell if you two don't."

Jace made a motion of turning a key in a lock over his lips, then winked at Cora Lee. "You've been here long enough, no one would think a thing about it."

"That is a topic I would very much like to discuss," she said as she set a platter of meat on the table along with a bowl of red cabbage and a bowl of something that looked like boiled balls of dough that held a faint potato aroma.

"We can talk about whatever you like over supper," Grant said as he washed his hands and dried them. He settled onto the chair at the head of the table as Jace pulled out Cora Lee's chair and held it while she took a seat.

When he was home, he'd taken it on as his duty to extend that small courtesy to her. In truth, he appreciated any opportunity to be close to the woman. She was friendly and warm, engaging and enchanting. If life were different, if he were different, he'd pursue her with every ounce of energy he possessed until she agreed to be his bride. Unlike Jude, coward that he was, who would likely hide out until Cora Lee gave up and left.

The problem with Jude's plan was that Cora Lee fit in so well on the ranch.

From their conversations, she had shared that she was an only child, born to older parents. Her father had owned his own shop where he made and repaired shoes, which explained why Cora Lee seemed to have some of the finest crafted shoes he'd ever seen. Cora Lee explained her family had lived above the shop in an apartment where her mother had created wonderful meals and a welcoming home. After her parents had died in a tragic streetcar accident, Cora Lee had been left alone. Although her father had taught Cora Lee his trade, no one would do business with a woman cobbler. She'd tried to keep the business going but finally gave up and sold it, along with the apartment. She'd moved into a boardinghouse, worked at a factory, and concluded she had to do something different with her life. An advertisement for a mail-order bride caught her eye, and here she was on their ranch.

Jace didn't think Cora Lee had much in the way of money, and he knew she had nowhere else to go, although he was sure Anne Milton would welcome her to her home. As one of R.C.'s good friends, Jace had been thrilled to see the blacksmith fall instantly in love with his bride. Anne was sweet and graceful and one of the nicest people he'd ever met. He'd stopped by a few times to see how R.C. was getting along. Once, Anne had insisted he stay for dinner.

The woman wasn't much of a cook, but she did make him feel welcome, and that made up the difference.

He could see why she and Cora Lee were good friends. The two women shared many similarities, and they'd both traveled to the West to marry men they didn't know. In Anne's case, she'd taken one look at R.C. and fallen in love. Too bad Cora Lee didn't have someone who loved her.

Jace stiffened as he thought about anyone taking her as a wife, anyone loving her. It made him feel antsy and annoyed, angry and irritated.

He refused, absolutely refused, to examine the reasons behind those feelings. It was just concern; like any man would feel for a woman under his protection. At least that's what he tried to convince himself of as he filled his plate after his father asked the evening blessing on the meal.

Uncertain what he was about to eat, he cut off a piece of beef that appeared to have been pounded flat and breaded before being fried. "What are we dining on this evening?"

Cora Lee pointed to her own plate. "The meat is schnitzel, the balls are potato dumplings, and we have red cabbage. Mae and I did bake bread today if you'd like a slice." She glanced from him to Grant.

"Let's give this a try," Grant said, shoveling in a big bite of cabbage. He squinted one eye, pulled a funny face as he chewed, and made a show of swallowing. Then he grinned at Cora Lee. "Very good. I don't know that I've ever had much in the way of German food, other than at the community dinners when the Müller family brings something to share."

Jace took a bite of the fried beef and found it to be both flavorful and tender. Surprised, he took another bite, then cut one of the dumplings in half and ate it, liking the texture and taste.

"Wonderful," he said, forking in another bite.

Cora Lee looked pleased, beaming at them both before she began eating her meal.

Jace and Grant both had seconds, then groaned when Cora Lee set the warm apple cake with butter sauce on the table.

"How about we enjoy a cup of coffee or tea and let our meal settle before we cut into that cake?" Grant suggested. "I'll stoke up the fire, and we can sit by it."

"I'll help Cora Lee with the dishes," Jace said, rising from his seat, wanting to moan at his overstuffed belly. He'd eaten too much, but it had all tasted so good. While he carried over dirty dishes, Cora Lee made a fresh pot of coffee. She washed and rinsed the dishes while Jace found smaller bowls for the leftover food and stored them in the outdoor cabinet. He grabbed a clean dish towel and dried the dishes, then put them away while Cora Lee wiped down the stove, counter, and table. Wordlessly, they'd worked in harmony, and that fact left him slightly unsettled.

"Finished?" Jace asked, unable to see anything else that needed to be scrubbed or put away.

She nodded. "I believe so."

He watched as she made a cup of tea, then filled two mugs with steaming coffee. He carried the mugs, following her into the front room, where the big fireplace cast off both heat and light, making the space cozy and welcoming.

Cora Lee curled into an overstuffed chair on the other side of an end table next to the rocking chair Mae usually occupied.

Jace was sure he caught a little sigh of pleasure as she took a sip of the tea, sweetened by a generous spoonful of sugar. She took another drink, then looked into the crackling flames of the fire. Mesmerized by the glow reflected in her eyes, Jace plunked into the rocking chair, unable to pull his gaze from her face.

"You especially thirsty, or did you bring one of those for me?" Grant asked, reaching toward Jace.

He looked down at the two mugs he still held. Embarrassed, he held one out to his dad, then leaned back and took a drink from the other.

His father shifted in his old leather chair, holding a recent edition of the Baker City newspaper in one hand and his coffee in the other.

Jace stretched out his long legs and set the chair in motion. If he wasn't interested in finding out what Cora Lee had to say, he could have easily closed his eyes and gone to sleep. Between the peaceful atmosphere, the warmth of the fire, and a full stomach, he was so drowsy he battled to keep his eyes open.

"Before my son starts snoring, was there something you wanted to discuss with us?" Grant asked, offering Cora Lee a questioning glance.

"I would like to discuss the real reason I'm here."

When Grant started to offer his rote reply about

being Jude's bride, she held up a hand to stop him.

"Please don't insult my intelligence any further, Mr. Coleman." Cora Lee set her teacup and saucer on the table next to Jace and leaned forward in the chair, appearing quite irritated.

The fact that she'd called his father Mr. Coleman instead of referring to him as Grant as she'd been doing the past few weeks let them both know she was upset.

Jace knew she'd gone into town with Mae the previous afternoon for a quilting bee. Maybe one of the women there had said something that she'd found distressing. He hoped that wasn't the case.

"I would never insult you, Cora Lee." Grant sounded apologetic. "If I have, I'm sorry. It wasn't intentional."

"Are you saying you didn't intentionally lie to me about Jude sending for me to be his wife?" Cora Lee spoke in a sweet tone, but her posture was ramrod straight. "You haven't been lying to me about him returning soon and going forward with plans to wed?"

"Well, lie is a strong word," Grant said, dropping the paper to the floor and slurping coffee.

"By all means, please explain it to me." Cora Lee remained poised on the edge of her chair, hands primly folded on her lap, looking like a fine lady.

An unbelievably angry one, but definitely a lady, Jace mused.

Grant turned to Jace, silently pleading for help.

Jace grinned and sipped his coffee. "Don't look at me. I didn't create this mess. I told you from the start to tell her the truth."

Cora Lee relaxed slightly and nodded once at him, as though in approval, before she narrowed her gaze and fixed it on his father.

Jace had seen his father face down Indians, drunken miners, a bank robber, and even an enraged bear without batting an eye, but he looked like he might start to cower at any moment as Cora Lee continued to glower at him.

Pleased he had a front-row seat to witness the mighty Grant Coleman practically shaking in his boots before an innocent girl, Jace wondered if his father would fess up and admit what he'd done.

While Grant appeared to search for the right words to say, Cora Lee didn't seem to have any trouble verbalizing her thoughts.

"Let me see if I can help," she said, sarcasm thick in her voice. "I do believe, Mr. Coleman, you sent for a bride on behalf of Jude without his knowledge. You pretended in the letters that were mailed to me to be him, then made up a multitude of excuses when he refused to have anything to do with me. Rather than be forced to wed a woman he has no interest in even meeting, he ran off and won't come back as long as I remain here at the ranch. Does that cover it?"

Grant had the grace to look chagrined as he slowly nodded his head. "I didn't intend to deceive you, Cora Lee. It's just Jude ... well, he needs to settle down, whether he admits it or not. I thought if a nice bride arrived for him, he'd take one look and ..." He shrugged.

"He'd what? Fall instantly in love, like R.C. and Anne? Is that what you expected?" Cora Lee asked. Her hands were no longer folded primly, but instead formed fists that looked ready to pummel something or someone.

"Yes. At least I'd hoped he would. I realize it was childish and irresponsible of me to do that, Cora Lee. I certainly never meant to drag you into the middle of a family problem." Grant sighed. "I do apologize for the deception. As for Jude, he ran off goodness only knows where. He's prone to do that, so don't assume his absence is due to your presence. He'll come home when he is good and ready and not a moment before."

"But he won't come home as long as I'm here. Correct?" she asked.

Covertly, Jace tried to shake his head at his father, but now that Grant had started confessing, it seemed he planned to tell it all. "That's what he said, but don't take it to heart."

"I see." Cora Lee appeared deflated as she slumped back against the chair, the starch suddenly departing her spine. "I suppose it would be best if I leave. Would someone be able to take me into town tomorrow?"

Grant choked on the sip of coffee he'd just taken. Jace hopped up and whacked him on the back a few times, until his father shoved his hand away.

"You don't need to dislodge my lungs, son." He turned back to face Cora Lee. "You can't leave, Cora Lee. We like having you here. Besides, if I let you leave now, Mae would never let me hear the end of it. Thanksgiving is this week, and she's counting on you being here. Several times, she's mentioned how much help you've been to her and how grateful she is to have you here at the ranch."

"But I don't want to be the reason your son, your flesh and blood, refuses to return home. No, I must insist that I leave—soon." Cora Lee looked down, but not before Jace saw tears glistening in her eyes. Everything in him longed to wrap his arms around her and offer comfort, but he wouldn't. He didn't have that right, and he likely never would.

He returned to his seat and picked up the mug of coffee just to have something to occupy his hands.

"Cora Lee, the thing you have to understand about Jude is that he says things he doesn't mean all the time. He'll come home when he's of a mind to, whether you're here or not." Grant looked to Jace. "Tell her, son. Tell her about Jude."

Jace had a strong idea his father only meant he wanted Jace to reassure Cora Lee her presence really had nothing to do with his brother's absence. He wanted to tell her about Jude. Tell her about his brother being a cheating, lying, scheming, thieving lowlife. But he wouldn't. Because in spite of all his brother's faults, his father could still see some glimmer of good in him.

With a great deal of restraint, he faced Cora Lee. "Jude will do what Jude will do. Nothing will change his mind. Believe me, I've tried more times than you could count. When he's ready to come home, he will, regardless of anything else. That might be tomorrow or a year from now."

Cora Lee's eyes widened, but she eventually picked up her teacup and took a sip, appearing lost in her thoughts.

Grant sighed and leaned back in his chair, picking up the paper he'd dropped earlier.

Jace pointed to a story on the front page and soon the three of them were discussing the apple tree growing in the yard of a well-known Baker City resident that had reportedly produced thirty-eight bushels of apples.

"That's a lot of apple cakes," Cora Lee said with a grin as she rose and went to the kitchen.

"And apple pie. And apple fritters. Apple dumplings. Oh, and applesauce," Grant said, with a teasing smile.

"I have the distinct idea you are quite fond of apples," Cora Lee said to Grant when she returned with a tray holding three plates with slices of cake. Once she served the cake, she refilled Jace and Grant's coffee mugs, then settled back into her chair.

"If I am to remain here, I do believe we need to reach an understanding." Cora Lee looked from Jace to Grant.

Fork nearly to his mouth, Jace returned the bite to his plate. "What kind of understanding?" he asked.

"I assume Jude has no intention of ever marrying me. Correct?"

"Well, we can still …" Grant started to say, but Jace tossed him a quelling glare.

"That is a fair assumption," Jace said. "Once he meets you, he might change his mind, but no one can make any promises about what he'll do. In the meantime, if someone else catches your fancy, you are under no obligation to Jude."

Grant nodded in agreement.

Cora Lee appeared relieved. "Be that as it may, there is still the matter of expenses you paid for me to travel here, as well as my room and board these last few weeks. I have a little money saved, but not enough to reimburse you."

"Cora Lee, you don't owe us a dime." Grant set his cake aside, rose from his chair, and moved over to stand in front of her. Much to Jace's surprise, his father got down on one knee, took Cora Lee's fingers between his big, work-roughened hands, and smiled at her, as though he was a beau about to propose. "I brought you here under false pretenses, even if I did have good intentions. Let's just say it was money well spent because the joy you've given us has been worth every penny. Fair enough?"

"No. Not hardly," she said, although Jace could see a smile tugging at the corners of her entirely kissable lips. "Besides, I must insist on earning my keep. Either you put me to work here, or I'll have to go to town and try to find a position."

"You have a place here as long as you want it," Grant said, patting her hands before he rose with a few creaks of his knees and returned to his chair. "As for you working, Mae always says she has far too much to do between Thanksgiving and Christmas. I'm sure she'd be pleased as anything to have your help. If that isn't enough to keep you sufficiently occupied, maybe we could hire you to do some shoe repairs for us. You did say you brought your father's tools with you, didn't you? I think every cowboy on this place has at least one hole in his boot, a flapping sole, or a worn-down heel."

Cora Lee nodded. "I did bring some of Father's tools. I will happily see to any repairs you need. I'd also be pleased to help Mae more than I have. From now on, please don't treat me like a guest, but a hired hand."

"You plan on heading out to the bunkhouse with the rest of the ranch hands?" Jace asked with mock seriousness.

"Absolutely not!" Cora Lee protested, clearly appalled at the idea. "Why, Jace Coleman, what sort of …" Quickly realizing he was teasing, she pressed her lips together and gave him a cool glare before she took a bite of her apple cake.

She sipped tea that had grown cold and looked from Jace to his father. "Did you see in the paper about the woman in London who decided it was her duty to walk around flogging people?"

"What?" Grant asked. "I must have missed that story."

Jace winked at Cora Lee and returned to eating the delicious cake she'd served, hoping she would forget about any intentions of leaving Elk Creek Ranch. He couldn't explain why, but it seemed as if Cora Lee had always been there, been a part of it. If he had anything to say about it, she'd never leave.

Chapter Seven

Cora Lee wiped her brow on her sleeve and glanced outside, unable to see if it was snowing since it was still hours away from sunrise.

She'd been up for two hours, along with Mae, getting an early start on the Thanksgiving feast they were preparing. In addition to feeding the cowboys who worked on the ranch, Mae and Grant had invited Pastor Ryan and Doctor Holt, as well as R.C. and Anne to join them for the meal.

The moment Mae returned home from helping Mrs. Garbaldi welcome a bouncing baby boy into the world, the woman had gone into a frenzy of cleaning and cooking. Yesterday afternoon, she and Cora Lee had pressed linens, then enlisted the help of Grant to extend the long table even further by adding in three additional leaves. Cora Lee had never seen a table that extended before and was fascinated to watch as Grant cranked a handle that spread the middle of the table apart so the leaves could be inserted.

Extra chairs were brought in from other rooms and a few from the bunkhouse, which Cora Lee polished. Then she and Mae set the table and added a centerpiece made of small gourds, dried ears of corn, an assortment of nuts in the shell, and pine cones. With more than a foot of snow on the ground, there were no colorful leaves or autumn flowers to be had, but when they finished, Cora Lee thought the table looked quite festive.

As Cora Lee rolled out another pie crust in the kitchen that already seemed too warm from the stove as well as their frantic activity, she hoped they wouldn't be too exhausted to enjoy the company once they arrived for the midday meal.

Mae had written out the menu on a sheet of paper along with a list of tasks. As each item was completed, she checked it off. When Cora Lee finished making the apple pies, one more task could be marked off the list.

Jace stumbled into the kitchen, rubbing sleep from his eyes before he appeared to pry them both open.

"What in the world are you two doing up at this ridiculous hour?" he grumbled, heading straight for the pot of coffee where it bubbled on the back of the stove.

"There's much to be done before everyone arrives," Mae said, sounding cheerful and excited.

"But couldn't it be done later?" Jace asked, pouring a mug full of coffee and taking a sip before he looked around the kitchen.

Not a single surface on the counter remained that wasn't already covered by something.

"If you complain, there's a pile of potatoes over there I'll set you to peeling." Mae waggled the spoon she held in her hand toward a large bucket full of potatoes.

"No, thank you," Jace said, backing away from them. "I will leave you to it before I get myself into trouble. Is there a chance we'll get breakfast today?" he asked as he continued moving toward the front room.

"Cora Lee made pastries yesterday. You and your father can have them with your coffee." Mae retrieved a platter covered with a snowy white towel and handed it to Jace. "Take that in by the fire and be sure you save a few for Grant."

Jace nodded to his aunt, but Cora Lee caught his rascally wink as he headed to the front room. She could hear him building a fire in the fireplace. A fire would offer a warm and welcome greeting to their guests. Earlier, when Cora Lee had returned from trooping outside to the privy, she'd gladly rushed inside out of the bone-chilling cold. Even in the short time she'd been outside, her teeth had threatened to begin chattering. She hoped the frigid temperatures wouldn't hamper their guests from coming.

Ever since she'd found out R.C. and Anne were invited to join them, she'd been filled with anticipation at seeing her friend. Of course, she saw Anne every Sunday at church and at the quilting bee Mae had taken her to, but that didn't give them much time to visit. Anne had invited her to come for tea, but it was such a long, chilly journey into town. Besides, Cora Lee had no idea how to drive a buggy or the sleigh she'd seen Grant polishing the other day. She supposed as the snow deepened the sleigh would be necessary to get to and from town.

Honestly, she hadn't expected there to be so much snow on the ground already. After all, it was still November. Regardless, outside it looked more like Christmas.

Yesterday, she'd noticed frost coating everything and a few icicles hanging from the eaves.

Grant had knocked down the icicles, afraid they might break off and fall on someone's head. Cora Lee could see his point, but they had been pretty as they glistened in the brief sunlight they'd had in the early afternoon.

As she finished assembling two apple pies, she went over in her mind what she planned to wear, how she'd style her hair and the possibility of getting to sit next to Jace. She knew it was ridiculous to entertain any notions about the man. He'd made it abundantly clear he had no interest in marriage or settling down, content with his life as a railroad engineer, and occasional cowboy when he was home on the ranch.

But the more time Cora Lee spent around him, the more she wanted to be with him. Something about Jace filled her with hope for her future—that everything would work out the way it was supposed to if she didn't try to get in a rush or orchestrate things herself.

She'd figured out within a day or two of her arrival in Holiday that Jude had no interest in her, and most likely hadn't been the one to write the letters she'd received. After being around Grant, listening to him talk and tell stories, she knew the words in the letters were his. What she hadn't been able to figure out was the reason why he pretended to be Jude or why he made excuses for his son.

Jace always seemed to withdraw whenever the subject of his brother came up. Because of how uncomfortable it made him, Cora Lee hadn't felt like she could press or ask questions. However, her curiosity was about to get the best of her. She wanted to know why Jude and Jace didn't seem to get along, and why Grant felt compelled to find Jude a bride. He didn't seem to be concerned about Jace or his lack of prospects for entering the fine state of marriage.

The thought of anyone marrying the handsome, teasing, gentle man made her want to cry. Or yank out the hair of the woman who would be lucky enough to become Jace's bride.

Jace was funny and smart, hardworking and thoughtful, and loyal. Every day that he was home, he did something to make Mae laugh, to ease her workload, and she'd seen him do the same for his father.

Cora Lee was glad she'd finally spoken up and forced Grant to tell her part of the truth. Nevertheless, she had a feeling there was more to Jude's disappearance than her presence at the ranch. She'd been feeling guilty about being there when it was clear she was not going to marry any of the Coleman men. The lack of marriage prospects was fine with her. She'd realized she wanted more than a loveless marriage with a stranger. She wanted love and romance, friendship, and a partnership. Things she was certain she'd never find with Jude, perhaps not with anyone.

At least now the family would allow her to help more, since she was supposed to be earning her keep. Mae had promised to give her plenty of work to do, and Grant had mentioned after Thanksgiving he'd like to have her repair a pair of his work boots.

It had been ages since Cora Lee had repaired any shoes, so she looked forward to testing her skill at it once again.

Today, though, was all about helping Mae prepare a feast that would fill the stomachs and warm the hearts of those who would gather around the Coleman's long table. The house didn't have a formal dining room like Cora Lee had seen in a few homes back East. The openness seemed friendlier to her, and it was definitely easier for the cook to set the food on the table instead of carrying it to a separate room.

Cora Lee removed three pumpkin pies from the oven, slid in the apple pies, and blew a stray tendril of hair out of her left eye.

"Here, let me," a deep voice said from behind her.

Cora Lee turned around and felt a decadent shiver roll over her as Jace gently brushed the hair from her face, then tucked an errant curl, produced from the heat in the kitchen, behind her ear.

"Thank you," she whispered, drawing in a breath tinged with cinnamon, sage, and a masculine scent she knew was uniquely Jace.

"You're welcome," he said in a husky tone,

then reached behind her, as though he was going to grab one of the pumpkin pies.

"Jace Jeremiah Coleman! You get away from those pies!" Mae warned, waggling her spoon at him as she kept watch over a bubbling pot of cranberries. "You'll have to keep an eye on him, Cora Lee. He has no control at all when it comes to pumpkin pie."

"Now, Auntie Mae, that's not true. I can control my fork just fine, carrying the next bite to my mouth." Jace tossed his aunt a boyish grin and reached for the pies a second time.

Mae rapped his knuckles with her spoon. "Out! Get out of the kitchen, or I'll heat up the rear end of your britches with my spoon."

Jace chuckled and stepped back. In a lightning-fast move, he leaned around Cora Lee, dipped his finger into one of the pies, then raced out of the kitchen.

Mae huffed in exasperation, but Cora Lee couldn't help but laugh.

She took a knife and smoothed over the pumpkin filling to hide where he'd stuck in his finger. "He's worse than three spoiled little boys."

"More like four," Mae grumbled as she went back to stirring the cranberries.

"Was he always playful like that?" Cora Lee asked as she set her hand to the task of making the dinner rolls.

"I didn't know the boys until after their mother died. My husband had passed on not long before then. He died in a wagon accident. My three girls and I were having a hard time holding things together, so we went to live with Grant and the boys. It worked out well because we all needed each other."

"And you lived here, in Holiday?"

"No. We lived in Kansas then, near the Missouri border. When the boys were nine, Grant convinced me we should all head out West. So that's what we did. We came across the Oregon Trail, like so many other families. Grant had talked to a lot of old-timers and people who'd been in the area. He decided he wanted to settle somewhere that wasn't going to fill up with people too quickly, so that's why we came here to Holiday."

"But how did your girls all end up living closer to Portland?" Cora Lee asked. She knew two of Mae's daughters and their families lived in Hillsboro, while her oldest daughter and her husband lived in Oregon City with their four children.

"Sarah met her husband on our wagon train and went on to Oregon City with his family. Florence and Emma both met their beaus when they talked me into letting them attend school in Baker City. The family they stayed with were acquainted with some fine young men, who swept my girls off their feet and moved them across the state after they wed. At least Flo and Em are near each other, and Sarah has her in-laws for company."

"You must miss them so much, Mae. Do you get to visit them often?"

Mae shook her head. "Not nearly as often as I like. I usually spend two weeks with Flo and Em at Christmas, then a week with Sarah in the summer."

Cora Lee glanced at Mae. "Will you spend the holiday with your girls this year?"

"I plan to. Jace will take me to the train in Baker City, and from there, it's not a horribly long trip. I'll leave on the twenty-third." Mae looked over at her and smiled. "Perhaps by then you'll be a new bride."

Cora Lee blushed but didn't comment as she stirred the scalded milk mixture she'd set aside to cool into a bowl of flour.

Mae offered her a teasing smile. "I know for a fact someone is quite smitten with you."

"Who?" Cora Lee asked, her head snapping up as her gaze met Mae's.

"I'm not at liberty to say, but it isn't hard to figure out." Mae gave the cranberries a vigorous stir, then turned back to Cora Lee. "And if you don't, I'm sure he will, eventually. However, if you haven't wed before I leave, and aren't comfortable staying here alone with the men, you are welcome to come with me."

"Thank you. I wouldn't want to impose on your time with your daughters."

"They would love to meet you. I've written to them all about your being here. Em is especially keen to make your acquaintance."

"I'll look forward to meeting all three of your daughters." Cora Lee began kneading the dough. "Do you have any photographs of them?"

"In my room. I'll have to show you later."

Cora Lee frowned. "I've noticed there aren't any photographs of Grant's family."

"The early photos Grant had of the boys

included his wife, Aria. He prefers not to be reminded of her. Once we moved out here, the opportunity to have photographs taken rarely arose. Although there is a photo of Jude and Jace when they were both about fourteen. It's probably in Grant's room."

Cora Lee stared at Mae. "They're twins?"

Mae laughed. "Yes, they are. Nearly identical. Didn't we mention that before?"

Cora Lee shook her head. "No. I do believe I would have remembered that detail." She continued kneading as she looked over her shoulder at Mae. "Do they really look alike?"

"They do. I've always been able to tell them apart, but some people had a hard time of it when they were younger."

"Why is that?" Cora Lee asked.

"They looked so much alike when they were young." Mae sighed a sad sound. "Now, Jude tends to swagger about like he's the most important person in the world. That boy has a hard look to him, whereas our Jace is just a good, upright man."

Cora Lee noticed how she referred to one nephew as "our" man and the other as "that boy." A hundred questions about the two brothers buzzed through her head.

"Mae, do you think Jude will …"

"Good morning, lovely ladies," Grant boomed as he strode into the kitchen, clearly in a good mood. "All those delicious aromas made me think I'd died and woke up in heaven."

Mae giggled. "Now wouldn't that be something? Pour yourself a cup of coffee. If you hurry, you might be able to wrangle a few pastries away from Jace before he eats them all. He's in the front room by the fire."

"I haven't eaten *all* of them," Jace called, causing them to laugh at the way he accented the word all. "But you'd better hurry, Pops, or I just might."

Grant quickly filled a mug with coffee, pecked Mae then Cora Lee on the cheek, and hurried into the front room.

Hours later, Cora Lee rushed to her room, took a sponge bath, restyled her hair, and dressed in a gown that looked more fitting for spring than Thanksgiving. As a finishing touch, she added the pendant that had been her mother's and returned to the kitchen. After tying on a voluminous apron, she helped Mae scoop the food into bowls or place it onto platters while Jace and Grant welcomed their guests.

Fourteen people sat around the table when Grant asked Pastor Ryan to offer grace. Cora Lee bowed her head and listened to the pastor's kind voice. As she said amen, she felt a leg bump against hers, then glanced up at Jace. He smiled at her and passed her a bowl of butter beans.

After a meal, which everyone declared was the best they had ever eaten, they all adjourned to the front room and engaged in a variety of entertaining parlor games.

Mae insisted they play a game named Forfeit. One person, Jace, was chosen to leave the room and was known as the judge. Everyone else was asked to place a personal item into a basket Mae passed around. Cora Lee tried not to giggle at some of the items the ranch hands added to the collection. When the basket came to her, she added her mother's pendant, knowing she'd get it back. She set it on top of a pocket knife, a marble, a length of leather string, a rabbit's foot, a lacy handkerchief, a tin of snuff, a pocket watch, and a small gold cross before passing the basket to Doctor Holt, who sat on her other side.

Once everyone had placed an item into the basket, Mae called for Jace to return to the room.

"Jace will choose an item from the basket and describe it. The owner must identify himself and pay a forfeit to win back the item," Mae explained, returning to her seat between the pastor and Grant.

"What kind of forfeit?" Anne asked, unfamiliar with the game.

"It is up to Jace to decide, but he might ask you to sing or dance or do something silly. If you refuse, the item is his to keep."

"Oh, I see," Anne said, giving R.C. a concerned glance. He bent down and whispered something in her ear that made her smile again.

"Shall we begin?" Jace asked, standing in the center of the room as he riffled through the contents of the basket. He chose an item and closed his hand around it so the owner couldn't see it. "I'm holding something perfectly round. It's smooth and made of glass, and captures the colors of a summer sky swirled with clouds."

One of the ranch hands stood. "That'd be my marble, Jace."

Jace grinned at the cowboy, who nervously

twirled the end of his waxed mustache. "I thought it was, Nolan. Care to tell us about the marble?"

"Well, my brother and I used to play with them when we were just little ol' grasshoppers. One year for Christmas, Santie Claus brung us a whole bag of marbles, and we thought they was the prettiest things we'd ever seen. I kept that one just to remind me of happy times with my brother."

Jace nodded. "That's a nice thing, Nolan. For your forfeit, you must walk around the room backward."

Nolan grinned, then proceeded to easily walk around the room backward. When he finished, he held out his hand, and Jace set the marble in it.

As the game continued, Jace didn't demand anything too trying from the players to reclaim their belongings, and Cora Lee relaxed.

"The next item makes me think of spring, with a flowing vine and pearly flowers," Jace looked at Cora Lee as he spoke, and she slowly nodded her head.

"It's my pendant."

"Is there a story to go with it?"

"Yes. It belonged to my mother. Her mother gave it to her as a gift when she turned sixteen. It was made by a jeweler who used to come to the bakery every morning and order a cream-filled pastry on the way to his shop. When my grandmother mentioned seeking a special gift for her daughter, he crafted the pendant in trade for a month's supply of sweets and fresh bread." Cora Lee thought of all the times just touching the pendant had made her think of her mother. "On her sixteenth birthday, my grandmother presented my mother with the necklace along with the story of how she came to have it."

"Then it is a piece of great beauty and great sentimental worth."

"It is," Cora Lee said, tipping her chin up slightly, determined not to let anything Jace decreed as her forfeit to embarrass her.

"In that case, I do believe, Miss Cora Lee, that you must make a face so silly, it makes at least three people in this room laugh."

Cora Lee thought it quite undignified to do so, but she moved by the fireplace where everyone could see her, then schooled her features into a face she could only picture as utterly ridiculous. She crossed her eyes, stuck out her lips, filled her cheeks with air, and wrinkled her nose.

To her surprise, everyone in the room broke into laughter.

"Well done," Jace said when he stepped behind her and fastened the pendant around her neck. While the laughter faded, he leaned close to her ear and spoke quietly. "It's as lovely as you in that beautiful gown of blue flowers."

"Thank you," she whispered, afraid to turn her head even slightly. If she did, she might succumb to the temptation to kiss Jace, and that would never do.

"Let's see who's next to meet their fate with the judge," Jace said in a menacing tone as she made her way back to her seat.

Anne was the last one to take a turn. For her forfeit, Jace requested she sing a song.

Everyone sat transfixed as Anne sang a well-known hymn in a pure soprano voice.

"Oh, please, Mrs. Milton, won't you sing some more?" one of the cowhands asked.

Anne looked to Mae, who nodded her head enthusiastically. "I suppose I could sing a few songs, but I hope if anyone else can sing, you'll join in."

For the next hour, Anne, Jace, and a few of the others sang hymns, popular songs, and even a few new tunes Cora Lee had never heard. Those who couldn't carry a tune happily listened.

As the last note faded, Mae and Cora Lee hopped up to serve dessert. There were pumpkin and apple pies, two chocolate cakes, an assortment of cookies, and a special pudding dish Cora Lee had made from a recipe her mother had taught her that was topped with sweetened cranberry sauce.

Eventually, the guests departed, each one expressing gratitude for a memorable day full of good food and friends. Anne offered Cora Lee a tight hug at the door.

"Promise you'll come for tea soon. Perhaps you could even come on a Saturday and spend the night. The Coleman family could bring you back to the ranch after church."

"That would be nice, Anne. I'll see what I can manage. Thank you for the invitation."

Anne hugged her again, then hurried out the door with R.C. The wind had picked up, and big, damp flakes of snow started to fall.

"Oh, I hope they stay warm on the way back to town," Mae said, slipping her hand around Cora Lee's waist as they stood at the door watching R.C.

help Anne into a covered buggy. The doctor and pastor occupied the seat in the back. All four of them waved; then R.C. snapped the lines, and his horse started off down the road.

"I think with that fast-stepping horse and the bricks we warmed for their feet, they'll be fine," Cora Lee said, moving back as Mae shut the door.

They sighed in unison as they made their way to the kitchen to begin cleaning up the mess. Jace stood at the sink washing dishes while Grant gathered dirty plates.

"You two earned a rest. Go sit by the fire while we finish in here," Grant said, making a shooing motion with his hand.

Mae grinned and tugged on Cora Lee's sleeve. "Come on, before they change their minds. I just got a new *Godey's Lady's Book* and want to see what you think about a pattern. I'm of a notion to make a new dress before I visit my girls for Christmas."

As Cora Lee followed Mae from the room, she glanced back at Jace. He tossed one of his rascally winks her way, warming her from the inside out. What a lovely, lovely day it had been. One she would long remember.

Chapter Eight

Jace climbed up the steps of the caboose and opened the door. The few men inside gave him a questioning glance but didn't try to stop him as he moved with purpose from one end to the other. He took in the neatly made bunks, the row of lockers on each side the men could use to sit on or keep their belongings in, a sturdy desk and chair for the conductor to use, a stove, and a table. The caboose, or crummy, as many railroaders called it, was a home away from home for the brakemen and a refuge for the conductor.

This particular crummy had curtains in front of the bunks, and a dog curled up on a rag rug near the small stove where a pot of stew bubbled, filling the car with a beefy, homey aroma.

Jace reached down and rubbed his hand over the dog's head. The animal licked his hand and wagged his tail in greeting.

"What's his name?" Jace asked, missing the dogs at the ranch. He'd taken Cora Lee out to play with them the day before he'd left. When Rusty and Ranger had engaged her in a game of tag, she'd laughed and fallen back in the snow, not even trying to keep the dogs from licking her face. The sound of her joy and the sunshine in her smile would most likely be embedded in his memories for the rest of his life.

Forcing thoughts of the lovely woman from his mind, Jace instead buried his fingers in the dog's thick fur and scratched him behind the ears.

"The dog? That's Brutus," one of the brakemen said with a grin. "And I'm Bob."

Jace smirked. "A real beast of a dog, is he?" he asked sardonically, giving the dog a playful thump on his side before he straightened and glanced around the caboose again. "You've got a real nice crummy here."

"Thanks, sir," Bob said.

"I'm Will. I don't think I've seen you around before. You new or just filling in?" another brakeman asked.

"Nice to meet you fellas. I'm Jace Coleman, and I'm filling in. My regular line is back in Eastern Oregon. I run a day line between a lumber mill, a mine, and a city that ships out a lot of gold."

"You don't say," Will said, propping his foot on one of the lockers. "What's it like, being on a day line? You have a little woman waiting for you at home every night?"

Jace shook his head. "Nope, but my father has a ranch, and I help out there when I can. It's nice to know most days I can sleep in my own bed and eat a delicious meal at a table that isn't on a moving train car."

"So, you're a real-life cowboy?" Bob asked, giving Jace a studying glance. "How long you been an engineer?"

"Going on two years. Started out as a telegrapher and worked every job there is except conductor before I was promoted to engineer. I know what it's like to be one of the shacks up there on an ice-covered roof in the freezing cold." He glanced up at the ceiling of the caboose. "I hope we have a smooth run."

"We do too." Bob shook his hand then Will took a turn.

Jace nodded to them. "God willing, it will be."

He turned and left the caboose, making his way through the various cars, studying each one as he worked his way forward toward the engine.

A few days ago, Jace had received an urgent telegram asking if he could fill in for an engineer who'd suddenly quit. Apparently, the man took exception to having a gun pointed at his head when a gang of outlaws boarded the train and robbed it. The company promised Jace to have a replacement engineer ready to take over within a week, so he knew he wouldn't have to be away from Holiday for long. But he sure hated being gone from home.

Christmas was less than three weeks away, and he loved being around the ranch during the holiday season. Aunt Mae had already started baking treats, and Cora Lee was adding delicious goodies unlike anything he'd ever tasted created from recipes she'd learned from her German family. His father seemed happier than he'd been in a long while, whistling while he worked. Even the ranch hands were getting into the spirit. Jace had seen two of the men hanging evergreen garlands across the front of the bunkhouse the other day before he'd left.

He missed being around Cora Lee. He hated to admit it, to even think it, but that woman had gotten under his skin, and if he wasn't careful, she'd be fully wrapped around his heart.

The idea of her being in his life on a more permanent basis didn't seem quite as unsettling as it had a month ago. Truthfully, he held a great deal of esteem and affection for Cora Lee. Far more than he ever thought he'd feel for a woman.

Jace had promised himself years ago he'd never allow a woman to tangle up his heart and thoughts like his mother had done with his father. Aria Newcomb had been the prettiest girl in town, and she'd known it. Her father, Abe Newcomb, had owned a big cattle ranch and she'd been the spoiled only child with her every whim indulged. Abe's wife had passed when Aria was born, and he'd raised her with the help of a housekeeper and a nanny. Aria had flirted with all the boys, but Grant Coleman had been the one who'd finally talked her into marrying him.

They'd wed and Grant had gone to work for Abe, a hard man who'd hated his son-in-law. He had passed away a few months after the wedding, leaving everything to his daughter.

A year after Grant and Aria had wed, Jace and Jude had been born, arriving ten minutes apart. Aria had taken one look at them, burst into tears, and proclaimed she would never have another child no matter how many Grant wanted.

And she hadn't.

When Jace and Jude had been six, she'd saddled a horse to ride into town to meet one of her many lovers. Grant had caught her, and they'd had a big fight, but she'd ridden off anyway, cutting across the ranch instead of riding on the road. The horse had stepped in a hole, breaking its leg. Aria had flown off and died instantly when she'd landed on her neck. Everything Abe Newcomb had once owned suddenly belonged to Grant.

Jace held vague, fuzzy memories of his father mired in despair after Aria had died. Then Aunt Mae and her girls had come to stay. Although they were older and sometimes bossy, Jace had loved his cousins like he would have if they'd been his sisters.

One day, his father had seemed to snap out of his grief and decided it was time to move away from the tragedy surrounding them at the Newcomb place. He'd sold the ranch, the cattle, even most of the belongings in the house, and had brought them all to the West.

Jace remembered when they'd arrived in Baker City. His father had liked the look of the area, and after two days of talking to ranchers and old-timers, they'd headed northeast to a section of land at the bottom of a tree-covered mountain. Jace had loved the smell of the pine trees, and he still did.

The town of Holiday had been founded later, after a big gold strike and the opening of the mine. The lumber mill had started soon after. Back then, before folks had begun moving into the area, the closest town had been Union, located to the northwest. Jace had always liked it when they'd gone in the spring because the community grew an abundance of apples and pears, and when the trees blossomed, it was an unforgettable sight to see.

His father seemed happier at Elk Creek Ranch than he'd ever been back in Kansas. Jace supposed part of it was because Elk Creek Ranch was something his father had built with his own two hands. The other part was most likely because there weren't any bad memories there of Aria or her father to haunt Grant.

Jace couldn't help but wonder if Jude took after their mother and grandfather Abe. He was flighty, temperamental, irrational, selfish, and sometimes downright mean.

The more he thought about Cora Lee's initial reaction to him, thinking he was one of the men who'd robbed the train, the more convinced he became that Jude had been the one she'd seen.

Even if he wasn't a wanted outlaw, it was just like his brother to run off and hide when there was something he didn't want to face, like their father arranging for him to marry a mail-order bride.

Jace still couldn't believe his father had done something so outlandish. He had to have known Jude would never agree to marry anyone. Jace couldn't help but think the woman who ended up with his brother as a husband would spend every day of her life regretting the union.

Gratitude flooded over him that Jude had taken off for parts unknown before their father had a chance to talk him into meeting Cora Lee. Just thinking about how horrible his brother would treat her—an upright woman with a good, kind heart who was innocent and amusing, and full of spunk— left him unreasonably angry.

Jace had no idea what his future held, but he was beginning to think more and more about it— and him—holding Cora Lee. The thought of kissing those lips that had tempted him from the first time they'd met made his mouth water. What would it be like to take her in his arms, feel her surrender, and love her with all his heart? He had an idea it might be like experiencing a little slice of heaven.

A loud thump drew Jace from his musings and back to the present moment. He watched a porter lower the ramp on the cattle car where he stood. If they were starting to load the animals, he'd best continue with his inspection of the train and get to the engine.

"May I help you, sir?" the porter asked, eying him speculatively.

"No. I'm Jace Coleman, the temporary engineer. Just wanted to look over the train before it was time to leave," he said, smiling at the porter as he hopped off the car.

"Nice to meet you, sir," the porter said, tipping his hat to him. "If I can be of service to you, just ask for Jimmy."

"I'll keep that in mind, Jimmy. Thank you." Jace made his way past the third-class cars. He hated to see them. The hard benches were uncomfortable, and the passengers generally were squeezed into them. In the summer, the smells from the car were nearly unbearable, with strange odors from packed lunches, unwashed bodies, and desperation mingling together in the heat. At least in the winter, the car kept warm with so many people occupying it. Too warm, most likely. Another challenging factor for those who traveled in those cars was the possibility of the car being left behind to make room for a freight car. A trip across the country could take twice as long for them as it did for the first-class passengers. He knew the travelers endured the hardships of the journey because they had to; it was all they could afford.

Jace walked through a second class, or day, passenger car. The seats were upholstered, but none of them were comfortable for sleeping, although some passengers somehow managed it. Most of the people who traveled in these cars were on day trips, not long journeys. Jace had seen everyone from miners and hunters to Indians and cowboys on the day cars. He knew the occupants of these cars often fascinated the wealthy passengers traveling from the East who'd never experienced western life. The second-class passengers were sometimes the first and only contact first-class passengers had with real westerners. Often, the men veered to the rough side, with guns at their sides, profanity lacing their conversations, and clouds of tobacco smoke filling the air.

He ambled into one of the Pullman sleeping cars, admiring the gleaming wood, the plush seats, and the atmosphere of luxury before he moved on, heading for the engine. When he climbed aboard, he found the fireman already there, enjoying a smoke before they headed out.

"Howdy," the man said, blowing a smoke ring above his head. "I'm Reed Barnes."

"Jace Coleman." Jace sized up the man as he shook his hand. Reed looked to be a few years older than him. From the missing finger on his left hand, he assumed the fellow had once worked as a switchman. Anyone who did that job for very long usually ended up missing a finger or two. "Nice to meet you."

"Likewise," Reed said, blowing out another smoke ring. "You new?"

"No. Just filling in while they hire a new engineer. I have a job on a short line in Eastern Oregon."

Reed nodded. "That sounds nice. My wife thinks I need to find a job closer to home, but this pays well, and I like seeing the country."

"From what I saw coming this direction, we'll have a lot of snow to get through." Jace had left the Holiday Express engine in Baker City in one of the other driver's capable hands and boarded the train heading east. He'd taken over as engineer when he reached Cheyenne, Wyoming, on an eastbound train, and driven it to Omaha, Nebraska. He'd spent the night there and was now taking this train all the way to Portland. If everything went well, an engineer would be at the end of the line, ready to take over duties as the train headed back east. Jace would catch a ride in the caboose back to Baker City, then ride the Holiday Express line home and be back in plenty of time to enjoy Christmas with his family. Too bad Mae didn't plan to stick around for Christmas, though. He wished his cousins would come to the ranch for a visit instead of his aunt going to see them. However, he knew Mae could use a rest after she took such good care of him and his dad and everyone else at the ranch all year.

Last he'd heard, Cora Lee hadn't yet made up her mind if she was going to accompany Mae to Hillsboro or remain at the ranch. He hoped, with just a little coaxing, Cora Lee would consider remaining at Elk Creek Ranch. He'd picked up a few little gifts for her when he'd gone for a stroll last night. They were safely tucked away inside his traveling satchel.

"Shall we get to it?" Jace asked, tugging down his hat and getting the train ready to roll away from the station.

Twenty minutes later, he glanced at his pocket watch, snapped it closed, and tucked it back into his pocket. They'd be ready to leave right on time.

Jace watched as the conductor headed his way. They'd met the previous afternoon. Jace liked the older man and knew his years of experience and wisdom would come in handy if they had any trouble on the trip.

"We're ready to go," the conductor said as he strode over to the engine.

"Aye, aye, captain," Jace said with a teasing grin, using a nickname often given to conductors. It seemed more respectful than skipper, which was another term often pinned on the men who were so vital to the efficient running of the train.

After the conductor gave a last call to board, Jace waited a minute, then released the brakes. The train belched steam as it rolled forward.

It had been a while since Jace had driven a train on this particular track, but he looked forward to seeing what this powerful new engine could do.

An hour later, he looked back at the fireman who was shoveling coal into the firebox like his life depended on it.

Jace placed a hand on his shoulder to stop his furious movements and gave him a curious look. "Is there a body buried in there I need to know about?"

Reed stared at him for a moment, then laughed and leaned on his shovel. "No. No there isn't. The regular engineer on this route likes to pour on the coal and pound the stack."

Jace knew some engineers used their position and power to make others work harder than they needed to, including the engine. But that wasn't how he ran things.

"You've got enough coal in there to take us to the next stop. Just so you know, I prefer to take things steady and easy, keeping coal and water consumption to a minimum."

"Now that's my kinda boss," Reed said, stowing his shovel, then climbing into the seat on the opposite side of Jace. "You say the word, and I'll shovel in more."

Jace nodded, and they traveled along like old friends. Reed told him about his wife and two children at home in Omaha. Jace shared about the ranch and life in Holiday.

Hours later, Jace was glad he'd thought ahead to bring provisions with him. The food at the stations along the way could be greasy, tasteless, overcooked, or undercooked. Once, he'd watched a woman faint when she'd found out the stew she'd eaten was made not of chicken but prairie dog.

Just thinking about the look on her face when she'd discovered the fact made him chuckle.

"You getting hungry?" Jace looked over at Reed.

"I'm always hungry," the man said, grinning. "You got something in mind for supper?"

"Yep." Jace pointed to a shovel he'd made sure was scoured and clean before he started his inspection of the train back in Omaha. "I tied a burlap sack with two nice slabs of beef outside your window. If you pull it in and throw the meat on that shovel, then stick it in the firebox, we'll have ourselves a feast."

"Boy, will we!" Reed opened his window and grabbed the burlap bag. It didn't take him long to find the tin of bacon grease Jace had tucked into the bag and let it melt over the shovel before he added the steaks. The smell of the meat sizzling made Jace's stomach growl. By the time the steaks were cooked to pink-centered perfection, he was starving. He told Reed to eat his first, then, while the fireman kept an eye on things, Jace hurriedly ate his steak. The beef wasn't as good as what they grew on the ranch, but it wasn't bad.

When the last bite of his steak was gone, he broke out a tin full of assorted cookies Aunt Mae had sent with him and held it out to Reed.

Reed took two cookies and ate them, then wiped down the shovel with a clean rag and hung it up to use later. In the morning, they could cook a couple of sausages or bacon on it.

The trip went smoothly as they headed west. Other than a few times when drifts of snow covered the tracks and had to be shoveled out of the way, the journey was uneventful.

Jace pointed out familiar landmarks as they neared Baker City. Reed asked him about the mines in the area and how far it was to his ranch. After the stop there, they headed north toward La Grande.

In the time it took Jace to travel from home to Omaha and back again, it had snowed a considerable amount.

As he neared a bend in the tracks, something made the hair on the back of his neck prickle. He'd warned the conductor, Reed, and the employees on the train to keep their eyes open for trouble. Not only had the Holiday Express line been robbed the day Cora Lee had arrived, but there had also been three other train robberies on various short lines in the area. Jace figured it was only a matter of time before the gang robbing the trains felt emboldened to try robbing a bigger train.

He slowed the train, cautious of what might await them on the other side of the bend.

"Anything wrong?" Reed asked as he slid off his seat and picked up his shovel.

"I'm not certain," Jace said, opening the window and leaning out, trying to see further ahead, but it was impossible. He eased the train around the bend only to find himself facing a wall of snow.

"More fuel!" he shouted and pulled the throttle wide open. The train lurched forward, plowing through the snow, sending it flying in a powdery arc. He expected to hit something hard, like a fallen tree or rocks, but the train chugged through the snow that had been loosely shoveled across the tracks to look like a large drift and came out on the other side no worse for wear.

He released a breath, then heard gunshots coming from behind them.

"Keep shoveling!" he yelled to Reed. The man started tossing coal into the firebox like his life depended on it.

There were more gunshots, but Jace didn't stop. He feared if they did, the robbers would completely overtake the train. He blew the whistle, emitting a sound that alerted anyone listening that there was an emergency.

Half an hour later, he pulled into the station in La Grande. As soon as the train screeched to a halt and he could step away from the engine, he asked Reed to keep an eye on things while he located the conductor. The porters helped a distraught passenger off a sleeper car. The young man had a bloody rag tied around his upper arm, leaning for support against an older gentleman as they made their way to the platform.

Jace ducked into the depot and asked the stationmaster to send for a doctor, then ran back to the caboose. He found the conductor there with two captured outlaws. One was unconscious and looked like he'd been dragged behind the train, with torn clothing and blood dripping from multiple gashes. The other man had a rag stuffed in his mouth, a black eye that was already swollen shut, and his hands bound behind him with a piece of rope.

To Jace's dismay, he recognized the man as

one of Jude's friends.

"What happened?" he asked as the conductor stepped over the prone robber and walked over to Jace.

"When you slowed the train down near the bend back there, eight men rode out of the trees and tried to climb onto the train. When you sped up, they started shooting. Bob managed to grab that one," the conductor pointed to Jude's friend, "and subdue him. He's got a mouth on him that would put a sailor to shame. The other one tried to jump onto the caboose, got his spur tangled in the railing and almost wound up under the wheels before we got him hauled inside. Will fired off a few shots, as did some of the more adventurous passengers. From what I could see, two of the worthless scum were hit, but the robbers turned tail and headed the other way when we caught these two."

"The doc is on his way." Jace glanced at Jude's friend. "I can identify one of those men. When the sheriff gets here, have him come talk to me."

The conductor nodded; then Jace hastened back to the engine. He hated for the train to be late for the next stop, but there was no help for it. He knew the conductor would have the station telegraph ahead that there was a problem and the train was delayed.

Jace didn't have long to wait before the sheriff arrived and asked him about Jude's friend. "He works up at the mine out of Holiday. Name's Boudry. Benny Boudry."

"And how do you know him?" the sheriff asked, giving him a studying glance.

"My brother is friends with him."

The sheriff's bushy eyebrows lifted, and the left side of his mustache twitched. "Was your brother one of the robbers?"

Jace shrugged. "I don't know for certain, sir. It's a distinct possibility. I've had my suspicions he's involved in something like this for a while, but I've not been able to prove anything."

The sheriff nodded and took down more notes, including the last time Jace had seen Jude and places his brother liked to lay low when he was avoiding the ranch.

"Thank you, son," the man said. He took a statement from Reed before he left.

While Jace spoke to the sheriff, the doctor had arrived and tended to the two injured passengers. He left with the sheriff, accompanying the two robbers since one of them required medical attention.

Relief flooded over Jace when he finally could pull away from the station and continue on his way.

"Whoo! That was enough excitement to last me for a good long while. The way you plunged right through the snow and kept your noggin engaged was some doings back there. I'd ride along as your tallow pot anytime." Reed grinned at him as he dumped a shovel full of coal into the firebox.

"I appreciate that, Reed. Thank you. I also appreciate your keeping a level head. I wasn't sure if we'd make it through the snow or end up buried."

"Well, you made the right choice," Reed said as they headed up into the Blue Mountains. "How did you happen to know one of those no-good skunks?"

Jace told him about Benny being a friend of Jude's. He couldn't help but wonder if his brother, at that very moment, was riding back toward one of his hidey-holes to avoid being arrested. Experience assured him Jude wasn't injured, or he would have known. During their childhood years, anytime Jude got hurt, Jace felt a twinge of the pain, too. He knew it was crazy, but he was certain that if his brother was bleeding from a gunshot wound, he'd know.

Then a thought worse than his brother being hurt hit him. What if Jude went to the ranch? Or went there and brought along his friends? The very idea of them being around Cora Lee made Jace antsy to head home.

He sent up a prayer for those at Elk Creek Ranch, and that Jude would change his ways. Jace had no proof, but everything in him proclaimed that Jude was one of those who'd tried to rob the train. No matter what it took, Jace intended to stop his brother before anyone else got hurt.

Chapter Nine

"This is exciting," Mae said, squeezing Cora Lee's hand as they boarded the morning train bound for Baker City. "We're going to have a grand day!"

Cora Lee smiled at the older woman, then glanced back at Anne who accompanied them. "I can't wait to explore the shops."

"I hope I can find a few things for R.C.," Anne said, taking a seat next to Cora Lee while Mae settled into the seat in front of them. The car was packed, and Cora Lee couldn't help but wonder if many of the other passengers on the train were also taking a jaunt to Baker City to acquire holiday surprises.

When Mae had suggested they go to Baker City and spend a day shopping, Cora Lee had declined the invitation, assuring the older woman she didn't need anything and didn't want to waste her money on a train ticket. Although Cora Lee loved the idea of exploring the town and spending time with Mae, she refused to waste a penny of her money while she figured out what to do about her future. Despite her many protests, Grant had been giving her a small weekly salary in addition to room and board for all the work she did around the house. Mae had turned over all the baking to her, and Cora Lee had also taken on the task of ironing, something Mae seemed to detest.

Rather than part with her limited funds on something frivolous, she knew the wise thing to do was to stay at the ranch and not be tempted with a shopping trip. However, Mae wouldn't take no for an answer. As a special treat, she'd invited Anne to join them, then purchased all their tickets, calling it an early Christmas gift. Grant drove them to the depot to catch the train and promised to be there when they returned later that afternoon.

Now that she was on her way with a day of fun ahead of her, Cora Lee fought the urge to bounce in her seat like a giddy child.

"Hopefully, those horrid train robbers have been arrested by now and won't be a bother," Anne said, adjusting her gloves on her fingers and settling back against the seat.

"Oh, I hope so too. Being held up at gunpoint once was more than enough to last me a lifetime," Cora Lee said.

"You poor girls. What a terrible way to be greeted into our area," Mae said, turning in her seat to look back at them. "I'm just glad you didn't let that experience scare you away."

"If we had, Anne wouldn't have met the man of her dreams," Cora Lee teased, bumping her shoulder against her friend.

"R.C. is a wonderful man, and I'm blessed by his love," Anne said. A dreamy look reserved for new brides softened her features before she glanced at Cora Lee. "What about you?"

"What about me?" Cora Lee asked, feigning ignorance and fixing her gaze outside the window.

"You've spent a great deal of time with Jace when he's not working," Anne said. "I think he holds a place of high regard in your affections."

Cora Lee shook her head. "That's ridiculous. Jace is just being nice to me because, well, because . . ."

"Yes, dear, tell us why?" Mae said with a look of mock concern.

Anne giggled, then looped her arm around Cora Lee's, giving it a playful tug. "It couldn't be that Jace has eyes only for you and you practically quake with emotion whenever he's nearby. It probably doesn't hurt that he's handsome and kind and strong and sweet."

"Don't forget charming. My nephew is quite a charmer when he wants to be." Mae smiled at Cora Lee. "Jace has been smitten with you since the first day you met."

Cora Lee had hoped and dreamed Jace might care for her, but it all seemed too unreal, too far out of reach. "But what about his declaration of being wed to the railroad and his job? He's made it perfectly clear he has no interest in marrying or setting down roots."

"Oh, bosh!" Mae exclaimed, waving her hand in a dismissive gesture. "That boy cares for you, Cora Lee. You mark my words. When he figures it out, there is nothing in the world that will keep him away from you."

Cora Lee blushed, and Anne laughed.

Her friend squeezed her hand. "You'd better be ready, my friend. When a good man, and one with broad shoulders and strong arms, decides to sweep you off your feet, you should be prepared for bliss beyond anything you could imagine."

Mae nodded in agreement while Cora Lee's entire face turned red. She wanted to lean over and press her burning cheek against the cool glass of the window but refrained. Instead, she looked to Mae. "What about Jude? He is the one I'm supposed to be here to marry."

Mae scowled. "No one expects you to marry that boy. Even if he is my brother's son, I wouldn't trust him any farther than I could throw him. Jude is too much like his mother's side of the family. It's best you stay clear of him, Cora Lee. He would toy with your heart and leave it broken beyond repair. I don't want that for you. Besides, it would kill Jace if Jude ever hurt you."

Cora Lee didn't know what to say, so she remained silent as the train headed through the snow-blanketed countryside. It was only a week until Christmas, and she'd so hoped Jace would have returned by now. He'd told her when he left that he'd be gone the better part of two weeks, and he had, but she missed him. She missed the sound of him stamping snow from his boots at the back door or the jingle of his spurs if he'd been out riding. She missed the warmth in his smile and the light in his beautiful hazel eyes that glowed with something she hoped was more than passing affection. She longed to hear the sound of his voice, the rich timbre of it as he spoke or sang. And she yearned to feel his presence near, to take a breath and inhale his wonderful masculine scent.

Jace was so much more than a friend, even if he didn't know it. When he returned to the ranch, perhaps she'd summon the courage to tell him how much he meant to her, how dearly she cherished the moments they spent together.

For now, though, she would push aside her indecision about her future, whether to remain at the ranch or try to find work elsewhere, as well as Jace's feelings for her, and enjoy the day.

"Did you happen to see the article in the newspaper the other day about the monument in Washington D.C.?" Cora Lee asked, hoping to divert Anne and Mae's attention away from her interest in Jace.

"I did see that," Mae said, twisting in her seat so she wouldn't have to turn her head so far to see them. "I'm so glad they finally finished the project."

"I admit, I haven't read the paper. What monument is complete?" Anne asked, glancing from Cora Lee to Mae.

"The Washington Monument," Cora Lee replied, knowing Anne hadn't been in America long enough to take an interest in certain topics that she might otherwise find fascinating. "It was constructed to honor George Washington."

"The first president," Anne said. "Did the article offer details about the monument?"

"It did," Cora Lee said. "The idea for it started

about fifty years ago when a group of people banded together to form the Washington National Monument Society. They thought a proper memorial for George Washington should be established and set about raising funds. They held a design competition, and Robert Mills was named as the winning architect. In the summer of 1848, the monument's cornerstone was placed amid a grand ceremony attended by thousands of people. Construction began, but the committee ran low on funds, and then the Civil War erupted."

"That was such a terrible time," Mae said, appearing sad. "I'm grateful those days are behind us."

Anne and Cora Lee both nodded.

"But what about the monument?" Anne asked.

"It seems when Ulysses S. Grant was president, he authorized federal funding to finish the monument. Work resumed five years ago. Sadly, between the time construction stopped and began again, the color of stone used in the marble of the monument couldn't be matched. It's darker at the top and lighter where the original construction ended."

Anne lifted an eyebrow. "And how big is the monument?"

"I believe the article stated it stood more than five hundred feet high. Workers placed a cap that weighed more than three thousand pounds on top of it a few weeks ago," Mae said. "I heard it is now the tallest man-made structure in the world."

"That's amazing," Anne said, smiling at Mae.

"I wonder how long it will remain the tallest

structure. It seems someone is always trying to be the biggest or the best," Cora Lee said, wishing she could someday see the monument that had taken fifty years to complete.

"I've heard rumors a large tower is planned for Paris. I wonder if it will be taller than this monument?" Anne mused.

"Wouldn't that be something?" Mae said, then pointed out the window as a small herd of deer raced through the snow, heading for the shelter of the trees in the distance.

Cora Lee still hadn't gotten used to the abrupt change in the landscape. It seemed one moment they were in the mountains surrounded by tall evergreens that filled the air with the scent of Christmas and the next they were in the midst of sagebrush and scraggly trees. Although, with the deep cover of snow, everything looked pristine and white.

She turned to Anne. "Do you have any gifts in mind for R.C.?"

"I do," Anne said, and their conversation returned to the upcoming holiday.

By the time they arrived in Baker City, it was almost ten. Unwilling to waste a moment of their precious shopping time, Mae led them toward the downtown shopping district. Their first stop, Mae insisted, had to be the dress shop.

"I need a new pair of gloves for my trip to see Flo and Em. If the price is right, I might even indulge in a new hat," Mae said as she pulled open the door and they stepped into a shop full of exquisitely-sewn gowns. There were also simple frocks and a nice selection of gloves, stockings, corsets, chemises, nightwear, and hats.

"Oh, my!" Anne whispered, squeezing Cora Lee's hand as they looked around.

"Mae McDonald! It's been ages since I've seen you," a beautiful dark-haired woman said as she sailed through a doorway at the back of the shop. The gown she wore, a glorious hue similar to crushed raspberries, looked expensive and impeccably styled to the woman's trim figure. "Will you stay for tea?"

"Of course, Maggie." Mae motioned for Cora Lee and Anne to come nearer, since they both stood at the door, gaping at the variety of merchandise. "I want you to meet two special young women. They both arrived in Holiday as mail-order brides last month. Maggie Dalton, I'm pleased to introduce Anne Milton. She married R.C., our town blacksmith. And this is our Cora Lee—Cora Lee Schuster. Grant lost his mind and sent for her on Jude's behalf, but we're holding out hope Jace will ask for her hand before some other fellow realizes what a treasure we have staying with us at the ranch."

Cora Lee again felt heat searing her cheeks, but Maggie merely laughed and gave all three of them welcoming hugs.

"It's so nice to meet you both. Congratulations on your nuptials, Mrs. Milton," Maggie said, then turned to Cora Lee, offering her a teasing grin. "Jace is a handsome one, with a good heart. Any woman would be thrilled to wed such a fine young man. I hope he has the good sense to propose to you."

Cora Lee found her tongue tied in knots and politely nodded.

Maggie took a step back. "I'll slide the kettle on to heat and be right back. Look around and see if there is anything you must take home with you today."

Cora Lee and Anne hardly knew where to begin. Anne finally wandered toward a display of gowns in Christmas hues of dark reds and deep greens. Fearful the temptation of a new gown would prove too much to resist, Cora Lee instead made her way over to the stockings. She could use a new pair, and they looked to be of fine quality. She just hoped the price would work with her limited budget. After searching through several pairs, she found exactly what she wanted, and the price was affordable.

Maggie helped Mae choose a pair of soft leather gloves with a warm lining. Cora Lee joined them when they ventured over to the display of hats. Mae tried on several, but Cora Lee liked the first one she'd tried the best. She smiled when Maggie picked it up and set it on Mae's head a second time.

"That's the one, Mae."

Although it was a simple style, a bow fashioned on the side with velvet leaves and roses made it appear quite elegant.

Mae turned her head from one side to the other, then finally grinned. "I do believe I must have this hat."

Maggie laughed and reached beneath a long counter for a hat box to put it in. After she packed the hat and tucked the gloves inside the box, she looked from Anne to Cora Lee.

"You two might as well try on something while you're here," Maggie said, giving them encouraging looks.

"No. All I need is this pair of stockings," Cora Lee handed the stockings and exact change to Maggie.

Maggie wrapped the stockings in a piece of brown paper and tied it with a length of green ribbon, then dropped the coins in her cash box.

"I would so appreciate it if you'd at least humor me and try on a dress or two. I just want to see how they look on a person instead of just my dressmaker's form." Maggie offered Cora Lee a pleading look.

"Come on, Cora Lee. It will be fun," Anne said, lifting a burgundy taffeta dress from where it hung, then grabbed a matching hat before Maggie escorted her to a changing room.

"I'll make the tea," Mae called, then walked into the back room.

Cora Lee looked through the Christmas dresses, but she was fearful to even touch some of the dresses made of silk and velvet.

"This one," Maggie said, stepping behind her with a deep red dress. The silk moiré seemed to shimmer in the morning light streaming in the windows. Snowy white lace trimmed the bodice and gave it a rich layer that was also feminine. "Try this one on. Please?"

Cora Lee couldn't have refused even if she wanted to. She followed Maggie into the changing room next to Anne's and quickly shed her serviceable woolen gown before pulling on the dress. Luxurious fabric skimmed over her skin like a lover's caress and made her feel like royalty.

Maggie helped her with the buttons, then disappeared, returning with a hat she set on Cora Lee's head at a jaunty angle.

"Come on out here," Maggie said, holding back the curtain.

Cora Lee could see Mae had returned and stood watching her with a pleased look on her face.

"Oh, you girls are just lovely," Mae exclaimed when Cora Lee stepped beside Anne, who was already preening before two big mirrors hanging on the wall.

"I don't see how Jace could possibly fail to notice you in that," Maggie said with a wink.

Cora Lee carefully brushed her hand along the side of the dress, loving the feel of the fabric. She glanced in the mirror, then took a second, longer look. She hardly recognized herself. The dress looked as if it had been made just for her. The color accentuated her skin tone and brought out the blue in her eyes. The finishing touch was the smart little hat cocked at an angle that made her feel sassy and witty.

She looked over at Anne and saw that her friend appeared as conflicted as she felt. They both knew they couldn't have the dresses, but they loved them.

Regretfully, they returned to the dressing rooms to change. Maggie helped Anne while Mae assisted Cora Lee.

"You look like an angel in that gown, Cora

Lee," Mae said as she unfastened the last button. "Are you sure you don't want it?"

"I'm sure, Mae. It's the most wonderful dress I've ever seen, but I can't purchase it. Not now. Not when my future is still so uncertain. I have plenty of nice clothing that is sufficient for my needs." Cora Lee knew the incredible dress the color of a Christmas berry had nothing to do with needs, and everything to do with wants. Oh, how she longed to own it. To wear it. For Jace to see her in it.

But that wasn't meant to be.

She and Anne left the changing rooms and followed Mae into the back room where Maggie poured steaming cups of fragrant tea and offered aromatic slices of gingerbread.

"This is so good, Mrs. Dalton," Cora Lee said after she tasted the gingerbread. "It reminds me of the gingerbread my mother used to make."

"Call me Maggie, and thank you for the compliment. I got the recipe from a friend. It just wouldn't be the Christmas season without gingerbread. This is actually the second batch I've baked, and I'll probably bake a third before Christmas."

"Your husband must greatly enjoy it," Anne said, daintily sipping her tea.

"No. I'm a widow, but my two dearest friends devour it like hogs."

Mae laughed when Cora Lee and Anne stared at Maggie, shocked by her words.

"Are your friends female?" Cora Lee asked, causing Mae to laugh all the harder.

"As a matter of fact, one is a lawman here in

Baker City, and the other is a miner and cattle rancher south of town. Tully and Thane have helped me through some rough times. We all came to Baker City together, my Daniel and them. Then we lost Daniel, and those two have been looking out for me ever since. Honestly, they're like overprotective brothers. Someday, they might even realize I'm all grown up and can take care of myself."

"Doubtful," Mae said, then took another bite of gingerbread.

The women chatted about the town, Christmas traditions, and people both Maggie and Mae knew before Mae declared it was time to move on or they would never get their shopping finished before it was time to head back to Holiday.

"I'm so glad you stopped in today," Maggie said, walking with them to the door. "It was lovely to meet you, Cora Lee and Anne. Don't be strangers. Please stop by anytime, even if it's just to say hello."

"Thank you, Maggie. We hope you'll do the same if you ever come to Holiday." Anne gave Maggie a hug, then stepped aside.

"I so appreciate your hospitality, Maggie, and thank you for allowing us to try on those magnificent gowns." Cora Lee hugged her new friend. "I hope you have a lovely Christmas."

"Oh, I will. Tully and Thane will be here, and things are never dull when those two are around." Maggie smiled and squeezed Cora Lee's hand. "You let me know when your wedding is to be held, and we can talk about a dress."

"I … uh …"

Maggie grinned. "If Jace is half as smart as he looks, you'll be Mrs. Coleman before you know it."

Cora Lee shook her head as she stepped back, allowing room for Mae to give Maggie a hug before they left the shop. "Merry Christmas," they called to Maggie as she waved at them, then closed the door to block out the frigid air.

"Come along, girls," Mae said, leading the way down the boardwalk. "We still have several places to stop."

Cora Lee purchased a sparkling crystal candy dish as a gift for Anne and R.C. without her friend seeing it before it was carefully packed into a box. She planned to fill the dish with marzipan, a candy her mother always made at Christmas. She knew Anne would love the dish and R.C. would enjoy the sweets.

For Mae, Cora Lee purchased a pretty set of stationery, since the woman often wrote letters to her daughters. Cora Lee felt bad that Mae didn't get to spend more time with her children and grandchildren. Perhaps, if Cora Lee did decide to stay at the ranch, it would mean Mae could spend more time visiting them. The Coleman men definitely needed someone around who could cook and clean and make sure their clothes were washed and mended. All chores she could easily handle.

It was the task of not losing her heart to Jace where she'd failed. How could she live there and love him as much as she did and remain only friends? It wouldn't work. It would never work. Not unless she wanted to be miserable. If she wanted that, she would marry Jude instead. Everyone agreed he'd be a horrible husband.

Cora Lee tamped down a sigh as she sat with Mae and Anne at a restaurant, savoring a late lunch. The chicken casserole, farmer's cheese, and canned peaches they ordered tasted delicious.

As they left the restaurant, Mae glanced at the watch pinned to her jacket. "We have an hour left before the train arrives. I'd like to visit the mercantile and get a few things."

"Certainly," Anne said, motioning for Mae to precede them. "Lead the way."

Together, they entered a well-stocked mercantile, where a friendly gentleman behind the counter greeted them, then returned to waiting on customers.

Cora Lee wandered up and down the aisles, stopping to browse through the selection of books. She'd noticed Grant seemed to enjoy an evening of reading when the work was completed for the day. She selected a book for him she thought he'd enjoy, added a few necessities such as scented soap and a jar of face cream to the basket she carried, and headed toward the front counter.

Mae was already there, paying for several paper-wrapped parcels. She smiled at Cora Lee, then glanced back at Anne who was intently studying a display of men's gloves.

"The ones on the left are the best quality for the price," Mae told Anne, then turned back to the man assisting her. "Frank Miller, this is Cora Lee Schuster, and that's Anne Charles Milton. Anne recently wed R.C. Milton, the blacksmith in Holiday. Cora Lee is staying at the ranch with us."

"It's nice to meet you both," the man said, smiling kindly as he finished with Mae's purchases and took the basket from Cora Lee. "Are you just visiting, or a new resident of Holiday?"

"That has yet to be determined, sir," she said, feeling at a loss because her future felt so uncertain.

"Well, I hope you enjoy the area for however long you are here."

"Thank you, sir," Cora Lee said, accepting her purchases from him after she handed him her money.

Anne rushed up to the counter with a pair of men's gloves in the largest size they carried, two books, a small bottle of perfume, and a few other items she acted like she wanted to keep hidden in the bottom of her basket.

"Mae, I was wondering if you could give me your opinion on a hair comb that caught my eye." Cora Lee led the woman over to a display, earning Anne's grateful nod as she paid for her purchases and Mr. Miller wrapped them.

A shrill whistle from the train made them look at each other as they left the mercantile.

"Right on time," Mae said, leading the way back to the depot. Packages and parcels filled their arms, so Mae went into the depot office to see if they had a box in which they could set all their recently acquired treasures. Anne departed to use the necessary, leaving Cora Lee alone on a bench outside that was tucked into an alcove out of the wind. She closed her eyes, drew in a deep breath, and let the fresh, brisk air relax her.

"You ready for Christmas?" a mellow, older

voice asked.

Cora Lee tipped her head back and looked into the twinkling blue eyes of the jolliest-appearing man she'd ever seen. Dapper in a pair of black and gray striped trousers, a dark green coat, and a red brocade waistcoat, he doffed his hat to her with a smile that seemed to carry the warmth of the summer sun.

"Mind if I have a seat while we wait for the train?" he asked, motioning to the other end of the bench.

"Please, be seated," Cora Lee said, smiling at him. She had no idea what it was about the elderly gentleman, but something in his countenance made her feel lighthearted and happy.

"Are you leaving home or heading there?" he asked, resting his hands on top of the gold-tipped cane he held in front of him.

"Neither," she said, then hurried to explain. "I'm staying temporarily in Holiday. I left my home in Cincinnati last month to … well, at any rate, things didn't work out quite as I anticipated they might, so I'm waiting to see where life takes me next."

"Do you like Holiday?" the man asked.

Cora Lee nodded. "I do, very much. I made a good friend on my travels here and she is now married and living in Holiday. And the family where I've been staying has been so good to me. I hate the thought of ever leaving them, but I suppose I must."

The older man's brow wrinkled. "Why must you leave them? They haven't wearied of your company, have they?"

"No, nothing like that. I just feel like I'm a burden to them, and ..." Cora Lee stopped before she confessed her real reason for needing to leave Elk Creek Ranch.

"And?" the older gent prompted.

With no notion of what happened to her ability to keep her thoughts to herself, Cora Lee felt like her tongue had taken on a mind of its own when it began spilling her secrets. "I came to Holiday to marry a man, only to discover his father sent for me without his knowledge. The man ran off and hasn't been around the ranch since my arrival, but he has a brother, Jace. He's kind and funny, honest and hardworking, gentle and caring. I do believe I've fallen in love with him."

"I see." The older man stroked his snowy white beard a few times, then looked back at her. "Before I dispense any advice, I suppose we should at least exchange names."

Cora Lee smiled at him. "I'm Cora Lee Schuster."

"My friends call me Nick." He studied her a moment. "Well, Miss Cora Lee. What seems to be the problem? The man you came to wed is clearly an idiot. And I'm not so sure his father isn't one for embarking on such a devious plan. Then again, perhaps things are working out exactly as they should."

Cora Lee frowned. "I don't think anything is working out the way it is supposed to. Not at all."

"You love Jace and he loves you. What else is there to worry about?"

A sigh rolled out of Cora Lee. "Jace has made it clear he has no intention of settling down. He's a train engineer and enjoys the travel and busyness of his job. Besides that, he hasn't said he loves me. Why would he? I'm nobody. An orphan without a place to call home."

Nick waggled a gloved finger at her. "That's a bunch of poppycock. You mustn't lose hope, my dear girl. It's Christmas. A time of miracles and maybe even a few wishes. If you could wish for anything, anything at all, for Christmas this year, what would it be?"

Cora Lee didn't need to think about what she wanted most. Her deepest desire rolled right off her tongue. "Jace. If I could wish for anything, I'd wish to be Jace's wife, but only if I could make him truly happy. Otherwise, I'd just wish for his happiness. For all the Coleman family to be happy and blessed because of how kind they've been to me."

Nick's smile broadened. "That's a fine wish, Miss Cora Lee. A fine and dandy one. You just hold it tight in your heart, and believe it will come true. I find a little hope, a lot of prayer, and a heaping measure of patience flavored with perseverance can make magical things happen."

Her lips turned up in a grin at the old man's fanciful thoughts. "If only it were so."

"Oh, it can be." He rose and bowed to her, tipping his hat. The breeze blew his thick white hair into his face. He chuckled, a deep rumbling sound that seemed to come from his belly as he smoothed his hair back before settling his hat on his head. "You keep on being the sweet girl you are, Cora

Lee, and I know you'll be blessed."

"Thank you, Nick. Are you catching the train to …?"

"Right there," Mae said, interrupting Cora Lee as she stepped outside with a young man carrying a large empty box. He set the box on the ground next to Cora Lee and tipped his hat, then eagerly took the coin Mae held out to him.

Cora Lee turned to introduce Mae to the elderly gentleman who'd kept her company, but he was gone. She hopped up and walked to the end of the platform, then peered around the corner, but he wasn't there. She knew he couldn't have just disappeared into thin air and run off without being noticed.

"What are you doing, honey?" Mae asked as she set her purchases into the box.

"Looking for Nick." Cora Lee scanned the people on the platform again, looking for the man. He would be hard to miss in his Christmas-toned attire.

"Who's Nick?" Mae asked with a frown.

"Nick? Nick who?" Anne asked as she hurried over to them.

Cora Lee gave one last look around as the train whistled and pulled into the station.

They were seated on the train, heading for Holiday before Mae turned to look at her. "Who did you say this Nick person is?"

"While you both were inside, an elderly man sat next to me, and we spoke for a few moments. He was very kind and jolly. He wore a green coat with a red waistcoat and carried a gold-tipped cane. His hair and beard were white and his eyes twinkled with mirth and joy." Cora Lee sighed. "I've never met anyone like him. I was going to introduce you to him, Mae, but when I turned around, he was gone."

Mae and Anne exchanged an odd look, as though they thought she'd made him up.

"He *was* there. And he encouraged me to not lose hope that my dreams might still come true."

Anne patted her arm and gave her a tender smile. "Of course, they will, Cora Lee."

"I'm sure they will, sweetheart," Mae said, reaching over the back of the seat and squeezing her hand. "Now, I want to know what you girls think I should wear with my new hat. The gown I …"

The rest of the trip, they discussed fashions, what Mae would take with her when she left to visit her daughters, the food they had yet to cook, and the treats Cora Lee planned to bake.

"I hope Jace remembers the grocery list we gave him," Mae said as the train slowed to a stop when they reached Holiday.

"I do too. If he doesn't, there will be far fewer sweets for Christmas." Cora Lee hefted the box with their purchases and followed Mae and Anne off the train. Grant waved to them and hurried over to take the box. R.C. was there and swept Anne into a hug that lifted her off her feet.

After the blacksmith had kissed her cheek and knocked her hat askew, Anne laughed and took her purchases from the box. She hugged both Mae and Cora Lee, then wrapped her hand around the brawny arm of her husband. "I had such a lovely,

lovely day with you both. Thank you for inviting me."

"It was such fun to have you two girls along," Mae said, beaming at them. "I hope we can do it again sometime. Maybe a spring trip will be in order."

Anne looked at R.C., who nodded his head in agreement. "Let's plan on it. Thanks again!" She waved and hurried off with her husband.

Grant held out his arms, and Mae settled her hand on one, while Cora Lee took the other. Together, the three of them made their way to the sleigh he'd brought into town.

"Do you need anything else while we're here?" he asked after helping them into the sleigh and covering their laps with a heavy robe.

Mae shook her head. "No. Nothing that I can think of. Do you need anything, Cora Lee?"

"No, but thank you."

Grant lifted the reins and smacked them against the rumps of the horses, and they were soon gliding down the road toward home.

Home.

Cora Lee thought it was such a wonderful word. Rather like hope. And that's what she clung to, hope for her future, as they traveled to the ranch.

Chapter Ten

"What are you going to do to fix this?" Mae asked, glowering at Grant as he sat at the table enjoying a second cup of hot coffee with a slice of pear pie.

"Fix what? Which *this* is in question?" he asked, taking a bite of pie, wondering what bee had flown into his sister's bonnet. She'd been giving him cranky looks ever since she and Cora Lee got back from Baker City. This morning, she'd elbowed him on the way to church so many times he was sure he'd have a bruise the size of a baseball on his side.

For reasons he couldn't begin to decipher let alone understand, she had insisted Cora Lee spend the afternoon with R.C. and Anne. Not that Anne or R.C. seemed to mind, but Cora Lee looked as bewildered as he felt when Mae shoved her off with the newlywed couple.

If he were R.C. and had a pretty little wife like Anne, he could think of better ways to spend an afternoon than entertaining one of her friends.

Grant forced his thoughts back to his scowling sibling. For no reason at all, she reached out and swatted him with her damp dish towel. If she'd actually put any force into it, it might have hurt. The fact that she popped him with the towel when he'd been thinking things he shouldn't made him wonder if she could read minds like she sometimes claimed to be able to do.

No wonder the kids all declared Mae had eyes in the back of her head when they were younger and got caught doing something they were sure she wouldn't see. He was starting to think there may have been some validity to their claims.

Mae had been the oldest and he the youngest in their family, so by the time he was old enough to know much of anything, she was already married and gone from home. It wasn't until years later, when his wife had died and her husband had passed, that they'd realized they needed each other and could be a help to one another. Mae had packed up her three daughters, sold what she could bear to part with, and moved to the ranch that had never really felt like his. His father-in-law, and then his wife, Aria, had made him feel like an unwelcome stranger so much of the time.

Grant had been sure once Aria had a baby she'd settle down and grow up, but she hadn't. It was as though the arrival of the twins had pushed her over the edge of reason. He tried not to recall the times she'd stepped out on him with someone else. Or the times she'd come home drunk and he had to put her to bed, cleaning up after her while trying to run a ranch and raise two active little boys.

From the start, Jace had been the easy child, the one who minded, the one who cared, the one Grant knew he favored, even if he shouldn't. Even though both of his sons were the spitting image of him, he could see so much of his cruel, selfish father-in-law in Jude. The man had been a terror on a good day, and it had been apparent early on that Jude would take after him and Aria.

Only a dunce would assume the boys never got into trouble. Grant knew they'd played pranks and done things they probably shouldn't have, just like any other young boys who grew up a little on the wild side.

While age had brought Jace responsibility, respectability, and wisdom, it was as though Jude had tried to regress to a wayward, willful child.

Jace, who was only a few minutes older than Jude, had both of his feet firmly planted on the ground. He had a good job and nice friends. When he wasn't working, he put in plenty of long hours helping at the ranch doing anything from cleaning stalls to breaking broncs.

Jude could sleep the day away, spend the night drinking and carousing, then come home and beg for money because he'd wasted his. He refused to help on the ranch unless forced, thought he was too good to hold down a job elsewhere, and treated everyone with disdain and disrespect. If Grant could believe the feeling in his gut, which was rarely wrong, he was sure Jude had gotten tangled up with a bunch of outlaws and had the audacity to rob his brother's train.

It wasn't any wonder Cora Lee had accused Jace of being a train robber the first time she saw him. Grant figured Jude had been the one who pointed a gun at her on the train, the one she'd bumped into and seen part of his face. At least his wayward son hadn't stooped to murder, yet. Or at least of which he knew.

Grant had about worn out the knees of his britches praying for both of his boys, but it sure seemed like Jude took up the bulk of his prayers.

Back in the summer, plagued by Jude's lack of interest and participation in anything to do with the ranch, Grant had decided something had to be done. He'd landed on the idea of sending away for a mail-order bride. It had seemed like a clever thing to do at the time, pretending to be his son as he corresponded with Cora Lee. Then the reality of the situation had set in when she'd been on her way to Holiday. What had he done? What kind of person would encourage a seemingly good woman to get mixed up with his troubled son?

Grant had waited until the morning she'd been due to arrive before he'd said a word to Jude. The boy had been out drinking and staggered in the door in the wee hours of the morning. Grant had been waiting for him and started pumping him full of coffee. When Jude had gotten sober enough to listen, Grant had explained what he'd done and insisted Jude go into town to meet Cora Lee when she stepped off the train.

Instead, Jude had grabbed his coat and hightailed it out the door. He'd come back to the house while Cora Lee had been napping and Grant had again tried to get him to see reason, but they'd both lost their tempers, and Jude had run off again. Jace and Mae had both seen him the next morning leaving the Ruby Palace, a despicable place he was sure Jude spent far more time at than he wanted to know.

Jude had returned to the house while they were at church, packed a bag of his things, emptied out the money Grant kept in the house, and disappeared. None of them had heard from him since.

Poor Cora Lee.

Grant knew she somehow thought it was her fault Jude wasn't there. The truth was, he spent more time off with his friends than he ever did at the ranch. It had been that way for years.

Why, oh why, had he thought a good woman would help Jude see the error of his ways? All Grant had managed to do was cause Cora Lee to feel indebted to them. After seeing Jace and Cora Lee together, witnessing the sparks that flew between the two of them, he'd hoped they'd fall in love. But it seemed neither of them were interested.

He couldn't stand the thought of Cora Lee finding some other man to marry. Someone who would take her away from Elk Creek Ranch. Grant liked having her there. She was sweet and kind and full of fun. And boy, could she bake! Mmm, mmm. He'd probably gained five pounds since she'd moved in with them, but Grant didn't care. He was enjoying her delicious cakes and cookies and pastries far too much to worry about his expanding waistline.

Grant knew Jace wasn't ready to settle down,

but he certainly wished he'd be a little more open to the notion. If he married Cora Lee, nothing would have to change. Jace could still work for the railroad. He was home most nights. Other than filling in the past few weeks, it had been a long time since Jace had been gone more than a night or two at a time. Perhaps he just needed to ...

An abrupt smack to the back of his head drew him out of his musings.

"Ow!" he exclaimed, glaring at Mae as he reached back and rubbed his head. She hadn't hit him hard enough for it to sting, but she didn't need to know that. "Are you trying to scramble what few brains I have?"

Mae grinned and plopped onto the chair next to his. "I thought maybe a jolt would settle them in a way they would start functioning properly. What in the world were you thinking, sending off for a bride for Jude?"

Grant shrugged.

"It has to be one of the stupidest things you've ever done, you thick-headed mule."

"There's no reason to resort to name-calling." He took a sip of his coffee and picked up his fork to finish his pie, but Mae grabbed the plate and held it far enough away he couldn't reach it. "Give me my pie. I'm not finished."

"You're finished, all right. I'll throw out every cookie and sweet in the house if you don't sit up and pay attention."

Grant narrowed his gaze and studied his sister. The look on her face said she meant what she said. Thoughts of the candies and cookies and special breads the women had spent hours baking going to waste caused him to lay down the fork and give Mae his full attention.

"You were saying?"

She sighed. "I don't know what put such a foolish notion in your head, to marry Jude off to some unsuspecting girl. A good girl at that. It was cruel on your part, Grant. Really, did you think this through? Of course, Cora Lee was smart enough to figure things out right after she arrived. In fact, I think she knew when Jude didn't come to pick her up at the station that something wasn't right, but that's neither here nor there. As far as I'm concerned, Jude is beyond helping except for the Lord himself intervening. Jace, on the other hand, desperately needs our assistance."

Grant sat straight up, feeling a sense of panic. "What's wrong? Is Jace hurt? Did you hear something in town? What's going on?" He jumped up out of his chair so fast it tipped over. "Where is he?"

Mae flapped her hand at him. "Sit down and calm yourself. As far as I know, he ought to be in Portland today. I'm hoping if all goes well, he'll be home tomorrow. Then, as you know, I'll be leaving. We need to come up with a plan to get Jace and Cora Lee together."

Grant righted his chair and sank onto it. "I've been thinking about that. Do you get the idea they like each other?"

Mae rolled her eyes. "Like each other? You've gone blind and dumb, Grant Coleman. Anyone with eyes in their heads can see those two are in love.

But Cora Lee feels some strange sense of obligation to Jude, I think, since he was supposed to be her intended, even if he wanted no part of it. Also, I think she's torn about holding Jace back in his career. She knows he loves his job. I think she's afraid to do anything to make him feel like he should be at home instead of out on the rails."

"That's plumb ridiculous," Grant said, planting his big hands on the table and pounding it once to see if it made him feel better. It didn't. "Jace can do his job and still be home most evenings and on his days off. It really is no different than any other man who works. Unlike the ranch where we're either flush with money or pinching pennies, depending on the year, Jace receives steady pay, and he makes a good wage. He can easily support a wife and family."

"I know all that. In fact, Cora Lee probably does, too. Jace is in love with her, but he's hesitant to admit it and relinquish what he sees as his freedom. After the way Aria treated you, I think he's wary of marriage. Marriage vows meant nothing to her."

"I'm well aware, Mae," Grant growled, hating the way the very mention of his wife made anger boil inside him. One of these days, he was going to have to face it, deal with it, and let it go. But today wasn't the day. "Aria was Aria, a product of Abe's raising. I should have known better than to marry her. She was probably on the back side of the church smooching on somebody five minutes before our wedding."

Mae raised her eyebrow, as if to pass on her

silent agreement.

"Aria didn't do right by you or your boys. That's not your fault, Grant." Mae patted his back as though he was a child. Oddly enough, he did take some comfort from it. "She was the prettiest girl in the whole county. You were captivated by her charms, and maybe a little by the wealth she and her father liked to flaunt."

"I was, but rehashing my mistakes isn't going to help Jace and Cora Lee get to where they need to be." Grant blew out a long breath. "I love that girl, Mae. She's spunky and lively and smart! Since she's been here, it's reminded me of the good times we had when your girls were still at home."

"Me too," Mae said with a wistful sigh. "I know she hasn't been with us all that long, but it's like she's always been part of the family. I don't want her to leave. But more than that, I want her to be happy. I want Jace to be happy. If they could be happy together, even better." Mae smirked at him.

Grant grinned. "What do you have in mind? How can we get them together?"

"It seems to me Jace needs a little competition for her affections to nudge him into action."

Grant nodded. "That might work. Who are you thinking? And don't you dare suggest me. I'm far too old for such nonsense. Besides, I just told you she's like a daughter to me."

Mae looked like she might whomp him upside the head again, but by some miracle, she refrained. "I was thinking more along the lines of someone closer to their age. I'm trying to do all I can to help, Grant, but you've got to work with me here. Put your head on straight and let's figure out a young man who would likely court Cora Lee if the opportunity arose."

Grant started rattling off names, and Mae got a sheet of paper, making a list. She rejected most of them, but they narrowed it down to three candidates. They purposely left off any of the ranch hands because they didn't want any uncomfortable feelings to arise after the dust settled.

"Read the names to me again," Grant said, leaning back in his chair.

"Pastor Ryan, the doc, and Murphy Brogan."

"Murphy's doing a good job at the assayer's office. I've heard a lot of people speaking highly of him," Grant said, taking a sip of the coffee Mae poured from the fresh pot she made after the first batch grew cold. "Pastor Ryan is a good man. Doc Holt is a steady fellow, caring, a bit distracted, but Cora Lee could do worse."

Mae stared at him again, giving him an exasperated look. "Focus, Grant. They aren't really going to court her, we just need Jace to think they are. If our girl gets married, I'm putting my money on Jace."

Grant smiled. "Shall I tell the pastor you've taken up betting?"

His sister tightened her hand into a fist. For a moment, he worried she would haul off and slug him. He supposed he deserved it for making this project take twice as long as it needed to, but he had such fun goading and teasing her, and she'd enjoyed it too.

"All we have to do is make Jace think they're

interested in her. It's not like he has to see them with Cora Lee." Mae tapped a finger to the side of her head. "It's all about perception."

"Remind me to never get on your bad side, Mae. You women ought to be the ones devising battle plans and running wars."

She offered him a smug look, then cut him another slice of pie. Greedily, he ate it in a few bites before she could snatch it away from him. He'd just shoved the last bite in his mouth when the crisp, clear sound of bells jingling in the winter air let them know Cora Lee was home.

Mae invited R.C. and Anne in, and the couple ended up staying for supper before they headed back to town. Grant gave them an extra lantern since the night was dark with clouds blocking out the stars, but R.C. had a good head on his broad shoulders and would get them home safely.

"Did you have a good time with Anne?" Grant asked Cora Lee as he settled into his chair by the fire and picked up the book he'd been reading.

Many evenings, they'd gathered around the fire. Grant would read aloud while Cora Lee and Mae kept their hands busy. Cora Lee often repaired shoes or boots while he read, claiming she enjoyed the task. Tonight, Cora Lee worked on one of his old boots with a worn-out sole while Mae rocked back and forth in the rocking chair, fingers flying as she hurried to knit another scarf. She still had one more to make if she hoped to give one to each of her grandchildren for Christmas.

Cora Lee glanced up at him and smiled. "I did have a nice time with Anne and R.C. He took us ice skating, and then we made snow ice cream."

Grant slapped the book he held against his chest and feigned indignation. "Snow ice cream? You had snow ice cream without me?" He looked over at Mae. "What is the world coming to with these young people making my favorite treat and not sharing?"

A giggle rolled out of Cora Lee. "Maybe we can make some this week."

"I'll hold you to that, young lady," he said, winking at her before he opened the book and began reading where they'd left off last night. Content and happy, he prayed there would be many more evenings full of joy and laughter in his home in the days to come.

Chapter Eleven

In a rush to return home after finishing his run in Portland, Jace caught a ride on a freight train headed to Ogden, Utah, and hopped off in Baker City. Since the train to Holiday didn't run at night and he didn't want to wait until tomorrow to return to the ranch, he appropriated one of the railroad track inspector's velocipedes and rode it to Holiday.

By the time he reached the Holiday station, the calves of his legs burned like fire from pumping the pedals while his hands felt permanently cramped from pulling and pushing on the handles that made the piece of equipment go. Although it wasn't as speedy as the train, it did cover the tracks quickly. The fact that he had to exert energy to make it go kept him warm until he reached Holiday. He left the velocipede at the station with a hastily-scribbled note to put it on the early morning train and return it to Baker City. Then he went to R.C.'s livery, saddled his horse, and rode the rest of the way home.

Jace swung out of the saddle and released a weary sigh when he reached the barn. He led Jericho inside, lit a lantern on a shelf by the door, then took care of the horse before he tossed his saddlebags over one shoulder and trudged through the snow to the house.

Half frozen, exhausted, and in need of a hot bath, Jace was more than ready to fall into a warm bed. He'd been awake for the past thirty hours and could hardly keep his eyes open.

As quietly as he could, he opened the back door and eased inside the kitchen. The warmth made his face feel like it was being pricked by a thousand of his aunt's sewing pins. He set the saddlebags on the end of the counter, walked over to the stove, and held out his numb fingers. He knew it was foolhardy to travel home in the dark and cold, but he'd felt a driving need to be there.

Assured all seemed normal, Jace released a long breath. He added more wood to the stove, set a few big kettles of water to heat, then removed his hat, coat, gloves, scarf, and boots. He lit a single candle and set it on the counter, then discovered a half-eaten pie beneath a dish towel.

"Merry Christmas to me," Jace muttered as he made a cup of tea. He placed a chair near the stove, then sat in it, feet extended to the welcome heat, and ate the pie while taking sips of the scalding hot drink. By the time he set the empty pie tin and fork in the sink, he no longer felt frozen from the inside out. While he wouldn't take the time or expend the effort to fill the big bathtub that hung on the back porch, he stripped off his shirt, dipped a clean rag into the hot water, and gave himself a quick sponge bath.

A startled gasp from behind him made him spin around, slinging water droplets from the rag he'd just dunked into a kettle and had yet to wring out.

"Cora Lee? What in thunderation are you doing up?" he asked, dropping the rag in the sink and taking a step toward her. Her hair hung in golden waves down her back, and she wore a frilly, lacy wrapper cinched at her slender waist. Glory be, but she was beautiful.

"I … I heard something and got up to see what it was," she whispered, moving closer to him. "How did you get here? It's the middle of the night."

He couldn't help but grin. "Yes, it is. I'm aware of that fact. I'll tell you about it tomorrow. For now, I just need to clean up and then rest."

"I'll leave you to it." She lifted her head and their gazes collided, connected.

Maybe it was the fact he was bone-tired. Maybe it was the worry he'd held for his family, particularly Cora Lee, ever since the outlaws tried to hold up the train yesterday. Maybe it was the lone candle casting an amber glow around the incredible woman who looked so warm and soft and lovely. Jace couldn't explain why he had such a sudden, irrefutable need to hold her, but he pulled Cora Lee into his arms and breathed in her feminine fragrance. One that filled him—flooded him—with a mixture of yearning and hope. Hope for the future. Hope for tomorrow. Hope in the possibilities that came from truly loving someone.

"Cora Lee," he rasped, sliding his hand along

the silky skin of her jaw before he buried it into the thick mass of her hair. It was even softer than he'd imagined as it twined around his fingers.

She didn't fight against him or try to pull away. Instead, she took a step closer and wrapped her arms around his bare back.

Jace felt like her fingers against his skin might brand him, searing clear to the bone. Rather than move away, he edged closer, eager for more. He brushed his fingers through her hair again, trailed his hand down her spine and back up, then cupped her chin. His thumb brushed over her lips. Lips that had tormented him since the first time he'd set eyes on her. Lips that had looked so kissable. Lips that he had to taste, to claim as his own.

Unhurried, he lowered his head to hers, brushing his mouth over her lips gently, reverently. Then a hunger, one that had been gnawing at him for weeks, exploded inside him. He had to taste her more fully, completely.

Afraid his amorous attentions would frighten her, he was shocked when she sighed in pleasure and returned his fervor.

Finally, after several long, ardent exchanges, Jace realized they were standing in the middle of the kitchen with the possibility of his father and aunt rushing into the room at any moment.

Although he hated to let her go, Jace knew it was time to release Cora Lee and get himself to bed before he did something they'd regret. After all, a sleep-deprived man standing half-naked with a beautiful woman in a shadowed room only possessed so much self-control.

"That's the nicest welcome home I've ever had," Jace said in a teasing whisper.

Cora Lee let out a sound that could have been a laugh or a sob; he wasn't certain. She rested her hands against his bare chest a moment, head tipped down. He could see her eyelashes shadowing her cheeks, looking like butterfly wings in the flickering candlelight.

Jace lifted her hands, kissed the backs of them, then moved away from her. He had to put distance between the two of them before he found it impossible to refrain from sweeping her into his arms and carrying her to his room. Or hers. At this point, it wouldn't matter a whit, except he would never do anything disrespectful to Cora Lee.

"I think we'd both better turn in," he said, backing away another step. "I'll see you in the morning."

"I'll be here. Sleep well, Jace," she said, offering him such a tender smile he almost went back to her. He even took a step in her direction but stopped himself. With a single nod, he spun around and hurried to his room, closing the door behind him.

As tired as he'd been earlier, he now felt wide awake. He finished undressing, crawled between the thick covers, and savored the taste of Cora Lee Schuster that lingered on his lips as he fell asleep.

Long before he was ready to awaken, the aromas of coffee and bacon penetrated his dreams of Cora Lee and brought Jace to a reluctant state of awareness. In no rush, he lifted his arms from the covers to stretch and hastily yanked them back beneath his warm cocoon of blankets. His leg and arm muscles felt like they'd been twisted into knots as he moved his limbs. He was going to be sore for a few days, but it was a small price to pay to be home, and especially to be there with Cora Lee.

He sat up in bed, recalling the passionate kisses they'd shared a few hours ago. Or had it been a dream? With his brain still foggy with sleep, Jace wasn't sure. He hopped out of bed, dressed as fast as possible in the chilly air, and hurried down the hallway.

When he turned the corner to enter the kitchen, he stopped and stared at Cora Lee as she bent over, pulling something from the oven.

"Morning, son," his dad said, giving him a hearty slap on the shoulder as he walked past him with a knowing grin.

"Hi, Pops. Anything new going on here?" Jace asked, following him into the kitchen. Mae stood at the stove, frying bacon and scrambling a pan full of eggs.

"Hi, honey!" Mae called over her shoulder to him. "I'm so glad you made it home before I have to leave."

"Me too, Aunt Mae," Jace said, kissing the woman's rosy cheek before he leaned around her to grab the coffee pot. He poured two mugs full and handed one to his father. "We'll have a whole day together before you abandon us for those rotten girls of yours."

Jace loved his cousins like they were sisters, and anytime they were together, they often traded barbed, teasing comments. He'd seen Flo and Em back in September when he'd filled in as the engineer on a train heading to Portland. He spent two days with them before he brought a train back to Baker City where the regular engineer took over again. He'd enjoyed seeing them and only wished Sarah could have been there too.

He was glad his aunt could spend time with her daughters and their families. He knew Mae missed them dearly and wished there was a way his aunt could be with them more often. But if she did that, it meant he wouldn't get to see her as much. Mae had been the closest thing he'd ever had to a mother— or a grandmother, for that matter.

Perhaps with Cora Lee at the ranch, Mae would feel like she could visit his cousins more often and not worry about the house falling apart in her absence.

Jace took a sip of coffee and looked over the rim at Cora Lee. She sliced something that resembled cake and arranged it on a platter. He wouldn't complain if they had cake for breakfast. And he really wouldn't mind a few more of her kisses either.

She glanced at him, then turned back to her work, but he noticed her cheeks turn bright pink.

Aha! So, he hadn't been dreaming. She had come to the kitchen last night, and those sizzling kisses had been real. He could still feel her delicate fingers on his chest and wanted, more than anything, to feel them brush over his skin again.

Aware the direction of his thoughts would only lead to trouble, he left the kitchen and went to the front room where his father stirred the coals and built up the fire in the fireplace. Jace looked around, pleased to see the family hadn't put the Christmas tree up without him. He couldn't remember when they'd started the tradition of a Christmas tree, but it had been about the time Sarah had gotten married. Maybe Mae had heard or read about it, but from then on, they always went out and cut down a tree from their property and hauled it into the house. The Coleman men acted like it was a bunch of fuss and bother, but Jace and his dad loved decorating the tree and tucking presents beneath it as much as Mae did.

Generally, they put up the tree a few days before Mae would leave for her annual visit to Flo and Em.

"Shall we go cut a tree down this morning?" Jace asked as he handed his father a few sticks of kindling.

Grant looked over his shoulder at him. "We've been waiting for you to get back. I think Cora Lee and Mae would love to choose it today. Mae hasn't said anything, but I think she was worried she'd miss out on decorating our tree this year."

"Well, we can't have that. Right after breakfast, I'll get everything together, and we can go as soon as the sun is up."

Grant added a log to the fire, brushed off his hands, and stood. "That's a fine plan, son. You know your aunt leaves tomorrow, so this will be perfect. Do you have to work today?"

"This afternoon and tomorrow, but then I have four days off." Jace would be glad for a few days of rest. He could have asked for more time off, but he figured he'd save it for another day. Because he willingly filled in whenever it was requested, worked extra hours, and did little jobs that weren't his responsibility, his boss had told Jace all he had to do was ask anytime he needed days off or help with something. Jace knew a day would come when he'd take his boss up on his offer.

"Great. It'll be so good to have you home for a few days." Grant placed a hand on his shoulder and gave it a squeeze. "I'm not sure how much longer we'll have Cora Lee here."

Jace whipped around and sloshed hot coffee over his hand. He ignored the spill on Mae's polished floor and the burning sensation of his fingers as he glared at his father. "What do you mean? Has she said something about leaving?"

Grant shook his head, looking distraught. "No, she hasn't mentioned anything, but a pretty girl like her, one who is unattached, a great cook, and sweet-spirited, won't remain unwed for long. Pastor Ryan and Doc Holt, and even Murphy at the assayer's office have all been vying for her attention."

Jace felt the muscle in his jaw tighten, and jealousy, so ripe and green he could almost smell it, ripped through him. "No. She's taken. They'd best keep on looking and leave her alone."

Grant gave him a surprised look. "Taken? By whom?"

Jace had yet to declare his feelings to Cora Lee. He sure wasn't going to explain them to his father before he shared them with the woman he loved.

There. He'd finally admitted it, even if it was only to himself. He loved Cora Lee. Was in love with her. Would do anything for her. Above all else, he wanted her to be happy, but he certainly hoped her future happiness could be found with him.

He'd been hopelessly in love with her from the first time she'd stood up from the table and accused him of robbing the train. After the kisses they'd shared last night, he knew there would never be anyone for him except Cora Lee. Despite his fears of making such a big commitment to a woman, of giving her his heart and hoping she'd keep it safe, he wanted to spend his life with Cora Lee. Even if it meant giving up the job he loved, he'd do it, just as long as Cora Lee would walk beside him for the rest of his life.

"Who is she taken by, Jace? Do you know something I don't?"

Jace growled and scowled at his father. "She's taken, and that's all there is to be said right now."

"Breakfast is ready. Cora Lee made a breakfast cake that smells divine," Mae called, interrupting their conversation.

Jace gratefully walked away from his father. He snagged a towel off the counter and cleaned up the coffee he'd spilled on the floor, then returned to the table just in time to pull out a chair for Cora Lee.

It seemed a lot had happened in the two weeks he'd been gone. But if any of the men in town thought they could sneak in and steal away the woman Jace hoped to wed, they better get their heads on straight or be prepared for a fight. Jace had no intention of Cora Lee marrying anyone but him.

Chapter Twelve

"It's gorgeous!" Cora Lee proclaimed, trying to run through the knee-deep snow to look at the tree from every angle. "This is the one. It'll be perfect!"

Jace gave her an indulgent look, then turned to find his dad watching him with a strange expression on his face.

"You heard the lady. This is the tree, son. Get to sawing," Grant said, handing Jace the handsaw he carried.

Jace used his hand and the back of the saw to scoop snow away from the trunk, then dropped to his knees beneath the fragrant fir tree and started cutting.

"Have you ever cut down your own tree, Cora Lee?" he heard his father ask.

"No. My father always bought one from one of his customers. The tree was usually small enough to sit on top of a table," she said. Jace could hear a note of wistfulness in her voice as she spoke. "But this one will be quite grand."

"It is a pretty tree," Grant agreed. "You did well for choosing your first one."

"Thank you," Cora Lee said. He heard her squeal with excitement when the trunk cracked and the tree fell with a loud whoosh.

Jace looked up at Cora Lee as she stood with her hands beneath her chin, excitement clear on her face. If she got this excited about the tree before Aunt Mae hauled out all the decorations, he could hardly wait to see her joy once it was trimmed with baubles and balls.

"I'll carry the saw," Grant said, taking it from Jace's hand. "You can bring the tree."

"So generous of you, Pops." Jace gave his father a derisive look, then stood, brushed the snow from his pants, and grabbed one of the tree's thick limbs near the severed end of the trunk. As they started the trek back to where they'd left the sleigh, Jace was glad they hadn't walked all the way from the house. With the snow as deep as it was, he wasn't sure Cora Lee would have made it far. As it was, her skirts were frosted with snow. However, when she lifted them to step over the creek, he noticed she had on a pair of britches underneath. He assumed Mae must have given her an old pair that had once belonged to him or Jude.

Thoughts of his brother made Jace's head ache, so he chased them away, determined to enjoy every moment of the time he had with his family before he had to head into work. He was only making one run to Baker City today, instead of the two he usually did. Then he'd work a full day tomorrow. He truly looked forward to time off for Christmas, especially with Cora Lee.

Nothing had been said about her leaving with Mae, so he assumed she hadn't changed her mind about staying at the ranch a while longer.

Jace studied her as she walked beside his father. She laughed at something he said, and joy shone on her face so brightly, it was almost like watching the sun rise over a cloud, illuminating everything around it. Cora Lee had brought so much happiness with her to the ranch. She could be playful and silly, fun and witty. She was also so easy to talk to. Her presence had blessed not only him but his father and aunt as well.

He'd been trying to figure out if his dad was serious about the men in town chasing after Cora Lee, or if the comment was meant to irritate him or maybe even spur him into action. Well, if his dad had some grand notion about forcing Jace to confess his feelings for Cora Lee, he was just going to have to get out of the way. Jace already had his own plans in place, and before Christmas Eve came to an end, he would know if Cora Lee felt the same.

Recollections of their interlude in the kitchen last night made him think she might like him, at least a little.

Cora Lee glanced back at him as he dragged the tree along, lost in his musings. She smiled at him and waved at him to catch up. The warmth in her smile and the tender look in her beautiful blue eyes gave him hope.

If all went well, Cora Lee would soon be his bride.

Jace used a rope to tie the tree to the back of

the sleigh, while his father helped Cora Lee in, then draped a heavy lap robe over her. Jace was surprised when his dad tipped his head, indicating Jace should sit next to her. Not one to argue with an opportunity he certainly appreciated, he slid in beside her and lifted the robe over his legs.

Grant whistled a rather boisterous rendition of a popular Christmas tune as he snapped the lines and the horses headed back toward the barn. Jace settled his arm around Cora Lee's shoulders. Without a bit of hesitation, she scooted closer to him, leaning against his side. Suddenly, Jace felt like joining his father in whistling. Instead, he adjusted the covering and tucked Cora Lee a little closer against him.

"This is nice," he whispered in her ear.

"Yes, it is," she said, then looked at him with her heart in her eyes. Her gaze dropped to his lips, and he was sure she was remembering the taste of his kisses like he savored hers.

Jace battled the urge to kiss her right then and there regardless of his father's presence. Instead, he gave her a gentle squeeze, then leaned back slightly. "Tell us about Christmas traditions while you were growing up. I know your mother was an incredible baker, and you've shared some wonderful treats with us. Were there other things that were special to your family?"

Cora Lee nodded, looking both disappointed and relieved to have a topic to discuss instead of intently studying his mouth. "We had many traditions we enjoyed. I already told you about our tree. Our apartment wasn't large, so there wasn't room for a lot, but we always had an Advent wreath."

"Like the one you made for our table," Grant said, glancing back at them over his shoulder. "It's been something nice to look forward to each week as we light the candles."

"Yes. I always looked forward to the first week of Advent, knowing Christmas wasn't far away." Cora Lee looked to Jace. "We had a nativity set my father's father carved out of wood. It's the one sitting on the bookshelf. Mae thought it would be nice if I set out my Christmas decorations to remind me of my family."

"It is nice, and your cherished treasures have been a welcome addition to our home," Grant said.

"I agree," Jace said, smiling at Cora Lee. "I was admiring that nativity this morning. Your grandfather was quite talented at carving."

"He was good at it, but from what my father said, it was something he did for his own enjoyment. As for other traditions, when I was little, I would place a shoe, all polished, outside my bedroom door for St. Nikolaus Day. In the morning, it would be full of candy and sometimes a small toy or two."

Jace offered her a curious look. "St. Nicholas Day, like Santa Claus?"

"No. St. Nikolaus Day is celebrated in Germany on the sixth of December. Nikolaus was a man who lived long ago, or so the stories are told. He sold all his possessions, gave his money to the poor, and spent his life serving the sick and suffering." Cora Lee smiled at Jace. "I suppose he is a little like Santa Claus."

"I think I missed out, Pops. Cora Lee got presents twice in December."

"I don't think you suffered for the lack of anything, son," Grant said good-naturedly as they neared the barn.

"No, I didn't." Jace grinned at Cora Lee. "Tell me more about the food traditions. Are there more treats you plan to make?"

She laughed, a sound that rang out as clear as the bells on the sleigh. "Yes, Jace. My gracious, but you and your father sure enjoy sweets."

"That we do." Jace gave her another light squeeze as his father stopped the sleigh at the barn. He helped Cora Lee out of the sleigh, untied the tree, and hauled it to the house. Mae stood on the step, anxiously waiting to see the tree.

"Oh, it's the best one yet!" Mae proclaimed as Jace shook the snow from the branches, then carried it inside.

While they were gone, Mae had shifted around the furniture so the tree could stand before the big window in the front room. Jace set it upright after he hammered a stand onto the bottom of the trunk, and then set the stand inside an old washtub. Mae poured water into the tub while Cora Lee went to her room, changed out of her damp clothes, and returned with a large box.

"What do you have there?" Jace asked as he removed his coat and gloves.

"Ornaments that were special to my family." She placed the box on the couch, lifted the lid, and carefully unwrapped a beautiful blown-glass ball. "This is a kugel, made in Germany, and brought with my parents when they came to America."

Jace admired the golden orb as it hung from a ribbon on Cora Lee's finger. "It's wonderful, Cora Lee. It will make the tree even prettier to have your fine decorations on it."

She smiled, pleased by his words.

Two hours later, Jace sat on the couch next to Cora Lee while Mae played the piano, and they sang a few carols.

He glanced at the clock on the mantel and sighed. He needed to leave if he was going to reach Holiday in time to work his shift. The thought of missing out on any time with his family, with Cora Lee, made him wish he didn't have to go, but he couldn't stay home when he had work to do.

That morning, watching Cora Lee take such pleasure in decorating the tree had filled his heart so full of contentment and happiness, he thought it might burst. She exclaimed over every little gewgaw Mae hauled out of the box where she kept the Christmas ornaments, asking about each one. Jace had memories tied to most of them, including a little train engine ornament Mae had given him when he was ten. It had been one of his favorite gifts and he'd kept it out all that year instead of letting her pack it away with the other decorations when the holidays had come to an end.

Before he tripped any further down memory lane, he knew it was time to go. He rose from his seat and glanced down at Cora Lee, who looked so peaceful and sweet. She fit so well into his family, into their home, it was like she'd always belonged with them.

If he had his way, she always would.

"It's time for me to head out, but I should be back in time for supper." He grinned at Cora Lee as he pulled on his coat. "Any chance you'll be making something sweet to enjoy tonight?"

"Perhaps, but only if you remember to bring home the groceries Mae and I requested."

"The crate should be in Baker City, ready to haul home with me. Although, I won't be able to carry it if I ride Jericho. Maybe I'd better take the sleigh."

"I left it out," Grant said, rising to his feet and pulling on his coat. "I'll help you hitch up the team. I'm sure R.C. won't mind if you leave them at the livery while you make the run to Baker City."

"No, he won't care. In fact," he turned to Cora Lee. "If you want to visit Anne this afternoon, I'd be happy to take you with me, Cora Lee."

"Oh, I'd love that, Jace, but I have so much I need to do today. I'd better stay here."

"I can see to the cooking if you want to go," Mae said, looking like she was about to yank Cora Lee to her feet and shove her out the door.

"Thank you, Mae, but it's not just cooking I need to see to," Cora Lee said, rising from the couch and walking over to Jace. She put a hand on his arm and looked up into his face. "Be careful and hurry home. I hope you have a good trip. An uneventful one."

"Me too," he said, disappointed she wouldn't join him. He couldn't help but wonder if she really was busy or just didn't want to spend time with him. When he got back tonight, he intended to find out. "I've had about enough encounters with train robbers and snow drifted across the tracks to last a lifetime." Jace wrapped a scarf around his neck, picked up his hat, and nodded to the two women. "I'll see you this evening."

"Bye, honey," Mae said, giving him a hug.

Jace opened the door and glanced back. Cora Lee smiled at him, and he winked at her before he stepped outside with his dad.

He was already counting the hours until he would see her again.

Chapter Thirteen

"I'll miss you every day that you're gone, but I hope you have a wonderful time with your girls," Cora Lee said, giving Mae a tight hug.

Mae patted her back, then kissed her cheek. "Are you absolutely certain you don't want to come with me? It's not too late to change your mind. Flo and Em would be so happy to meet you, and Em has plenty of room for you at her house."

Cora Lee hugged Mae again, then stepped back." I'm certain, Mae. You go on and enjoy time with your daughters. If I'm not here, who would make sure Jace and Grant are properly fed and Santa Claus comes?"

Mae laughed. "As ornery as these two are, Santa will likely leave coal in their stockings."

"Hey!" Jace objected, grinning at his aunt as he shrugged into his coat, then tamped his feet into his work boots. "I'm on Santa's good boy list."

"Me, too," Grant said, snatching a handful of cookies from the jar on the counter and handing half of them to Jace.

"Stealing cookies and fibbing won't earn you any favors with Santa," Mae warned, shaking her finger at her brother.

Grant chuckled, kissed Cora Lee's cheek, then went out the door. They'd already loaded the two trunks Mae was taking with her, one full to the brim with gifts.

"Don't let these two work you too hard while I'm gone. In fact, I think you should take a few days just to relax, Cora Lee. You've more than earned it." Mae smiled at her again, then scurried out the door.

Jace wound a scarf around his neck and picked up his hat. "Are you sure you don't want to come into town with us? Anne and R.C. would be happy to have you visit them today."

"I'm sure, Jace. I'll be fine here."

"But the house will be quiet and lonesome with everyone gone."

Cora Lee had been looking forward to a little quiet time to finish her Christmas gifts. She didn't mind being alone, although she would miss all of them, especially Jace.

Last night, he'd asked her to stay up with him awhile after Grant and Mae had already gone to bed. For an hour, they'd sat side by side near the fire and just talked like old friends. Cora Lee had enjoyed every moment of it. Then Jace had kissed her with such tenderness, it had left her weak-kneed and wishing for more. He hadn't said the words, but she was sure he loved her as much as she loved him.

At least she assumed that fiery look in his eyes

meant he cared for her. She'd glanced up as they were eating breakfast and caught him watching her. One gaze into his incredible hazel eyes had left her warm and languid and feeling loved. It was almost like a caress, the way he'd smiled at her earlier, much like he was now.

"I don't mind a little quiet now and then." Cora Lee reached out and squeezed his hand. "Have a good trip today. It's nice Grant can ride to Baker City on the train with Mae."

"I'm glad he's getting away for the day. He doesn't do that very often. And we'll be able to eat lunch together before I have to make my second run. But we'll be back in time for supper." Jace grinned at her. "Any delicious treats planned for tonight? The apple thing you baked yesterday was delicious."

"Apple kuchen, and I'm glad you enjoyed it. I plan to make stollen today, and more cookies."

"Stollen? What's that?" Jace asked as he pulled on his gloves.

"A sweet bread with dried fruit and nuts. It's something my family made every year. The recipe comes from my great-grandmother and the family bakery."

"Then I can't wait to taste it." Jace pulled her into a hug and brushed his lips over hers before he leaned back. "I sure enjoyed talking with you last night. Maybe you'd be willing to sit up with me for a while again tonight?"

"I'd like that, Jace. So much." Cora Lee adjusted his scarf, using it as an excuse to touch him, then kissed his cheek. "Be safe and have a grand day."

"You do the same, my sweet Cora Lee." He lifted her hands to his lips and kissed the backs of her fingers. "I'll see you tonight."

Cora Lee stood at the door and waved as Jace ran out to the sleigh where Grant and Mae waited, then climbed onto the seat. He returned her wave as the team started toward town. Before she closed the door, she waved at the ranch hands who worked around the barn and bunkhouse. She knew if she needed anything, they would help her.

She returned inside and closed the door, shutting out the nippy air. Although the glimmer of sunlight on the horizon hinted it would be a nice day, the temperatures were below freezing.

After she washed the breakfast dishes and set the kitchen to rights, Cora Lee baked four loaves of stollen bread and made two batches of cookies. With her baking completed, she went to her room and brought her gift for Jace to the kitchen where it was warm. Not long after she'd arrived at the ranch, he'd mentioned he needed a new pair of boots, so she'd gotten out the tools she'd brought along and set about making a pair. Grant and Mae both knew about the gift because of the many evenings she'd sat by the fire as she worked on them. It made her sad, yet comforted her too, to hold the tools that had been worn smooth by her father's hands.

Cora Lee had loved learning his trade and had a talent for it, but no one had seemed interested in buying shoes made by a woman. She thought it was ridiculous, but maybe someday the prejudice would change. For now, she could at least use her talents creatively for those she loved.

And she did love Jace. With all her heart.

The more time she spent with him, the more she wanted to be with him. Always. Her conversation with the older man at the train station in Baker City came back to her. If she could make one wish for Christmas, it would be for Jace to love her, to ask her to marry him. How glorious it would be to be his wife, his cherished bride.

But Cora Lee still felt uncertain. Until Jace made any declaration, she refused to let her dreams carry away her good sense.

As she worked to put the finishing touches on the last boot, she wondered if she'd imagined the old man with the snowy hair and beard or if he'd really been there. In spite of her doubts, she was convinced he was real. A kind old soul with the happiest countenance she'd ever seen.

Perhaps he'd be at the station today and Mae would see him.

Cora Lee hoped the woman had a pleasant trip to Hillsboro where Flo and Em both resided. She'd discovered the two sisters lived just a few houses apart on the same street. If the women were anything like their mother, she imagined they were full of life, laughed easily, and had caring hearts. Often, when she was a child, Cora Lee had wished for a sister or a brother. She'd learned when she was older that her mother had miscarried multiple times, unable to have more children. It must have been so hard on her parents to long for more children and not be able to welcome more to the family.

She hoped she'd brought them joy and hadn't

been too much of a trial to them. In her mind, they'd been a happy family who had truly enjoyed being together. Her father had always closed his shop for thirty minutes at noon each work day to come upstairs and eat lunch together. Some of her favorite memories had been when she'd been out of school for the summer, or during the holidays, when she could spend time in the shop that had carried the wonderful, deep aromas of leather.

Cora Lee smiled, recalling how Jace's unique scent that carried a hint of leather was one of the things she'd noticed about him. Then she decided it didn't matter. Not his scent or his clothes or the fact that he had a good job that paid well. What mattered was Jace. He was a good man, a caring man, one who was thoughtful and generous and tender yet tough. He was the sort of man a woman dreams of finding and holding onto for the rest of her life.

Not that she needed a man to hold her up. Not in the least. She wanted, quite desperately, though, to go through life with Jace holding her hand and her heart.

She sat back and looked at the boots, thrilled with how they'd turned out. She'd used a worn-out pair of boots that had been Jace's to measure his foot size and shape. The leather she'd chosen to use was pliable yet sturdy, and the sole should last for many years. After taking a rag and polish to the boots, they were soon shiny. She'd set aside a box to wrap them in and saved a large sheet of brown paper Mae had told her she could have. The Christmas carol she hummed as she wrapped the box and tied it with a bright red ribbon broke up the silence of the house. When she finished, she set the gift beneath the tree, then adjusted a few of the gifts that were propped against the washtub that held the tree.

Cora Lee decided the tree needed to be watered and saw to the task; then she made a beef sandwich and sliced a pear to enjoy with her lunch. She'd been amazed the first time Mae had taken her into the cellar, where there were baskets brimming with fruits and vegetables as well as shelves filled with canned goods. Mae told her canning season was a hectic time for her as she worked to preserve as much of her garden produce as possible. Rows of jars filled with green beans, peas, tomatoes, pickles, and corn sat alongside jars full of peaches, cherries, pears, and an assortment of jellies made from wild berries that grew in the mountains, as well as strawberries Mae had planted in the garden. There were also canned jars of beef and a big crock held sausages layered in lard to preserve it.

The abundance of food available at the ranch was something she still hadn't grown accustomed to. She'd never once gone hungry, but there were times when the Schuster household didn't have much money, so the food they could afford was simple at best.

Regardless of their finances, at Christmas, there had always been many delicious treats. Dishes her mother had taught her to make. Traditional recipes that drew Cora Lee close to her parents and their home in Germany.

As she ate, she wondered what it was like for her mother and father, leaving the only place they'd ever known to venture across an ocean and begin a new life. She knew they'd worked hard to learn English and speak as plainly as possible. Her mother had insisted early on that Cora Lee speak English, but her father had taught her German until she was fluent in both.

Her parents had endured many hardships, many disappointments, but they'd also had many triumphs too. Through it all, she felt they'd given her an example of remaining cheerful, ever hopeful, that everything would work out for the best.

For the most part, it had.

Cora Lee set down her sandwich and took a moment to offer a prayer of thanks for her parents, for being raised by a loving couple who gave her a solid foundation in life.

After she finished eating and washed the few dishes she'd dirtied, she took a beef roast from the cold storage cupboard on the porch where she'd had it resting in a bowl of marinade for three days. Each day she'd turned it, making sure all sides were covered, soaking up the sauce she'd concocted of spices, chopped carrots, onions, vinegar, and grape juice. Although dinner was hours away, she set the meat in a deep roasting pan and slid it into the oven to roast all afternoon. By supper time, the meat would be incredibly tender and bursting with flavor. She planned to serve cabbage and potato dumplings with it. Both Jace and Grant seemed to love anything made with potatoes.

She cleaned the kitchen again before making a hasty trip outside to the necessary. Cora Lee rubbed her hands on her chilled arms as she scurried back inside, closed the door, and stoked the fire in the fireplace in the front room.

Ready for a rest, she sat in Mae's rocker and finished stitching a bookmark she'd made for Grant. He used a tattered scrap of paper to mark his place when he read. Cora Lee had embroidered a cross with a few stalks of wheat on a thick piece of muslin, then added a verse from the twenty-third Psalm that seemed to be one of his favorites. After finishing the edges, she added a tassel at one end. She wrapped it in a piece of tissue paper and fastened it with a small piece of green ribbon. She set it on top of the book she'd already wrapped for Grant and placed it beneath the tree.

She smiled, thinking of how surprised Jace and Grant would be Christmas morning when they awoke to find there were stockings hanging on the mantel for them, filled with nuts, oranges, wrapped chocolates, and new gloves. Mae had taken care of filling the stockings, then shown Cora Lee where she'd hidden them in a bottom drawer in the empty guest room.

With all of her gifts wrapped and beneath the tree, Cora Lee whipped up chocolate pudding, one of Jace's favorites, and spooned it into bowls, then set them inside the cold storage cupboard.

In need of something to keep her busy, she removed the sheets from Mae's bed and washed them so they'd be fresh when the woman returned. A line Mae had stretched behind the kitchen stove was the perfect place for laundry to dry when it couldn't be hung outside.

She'd just started out of the kitchen when

someone banged on the back door. Changing direction, she headed toward it but hadn't yet reached it when it swung open and one of the cowboys who worked for Grant poked his head inside.

"Hello, Nolan. How are you today?" she asked with what she hoped was a welcoming smile.

"Fine, Miss Cora Lee. Something spooked the cattle, and they stampeded through the fence, knocking it into splinters. They've run off in every direction. Until we get it all sorted out, I thought it might be best to tell you to stay inside the house, in case you were planning on going out for a walk or something."

"Oh, gracious!" Cora Lee offered him a worried glance. "Is there anything I can do to help?"

"No, miss, but thank you. Just stay inside where it's safe." Nolan tipped his hat to her, then closed the door.

Cora Lee ran to the front of the house, opened the door, and stepped onto the porch. Although she couldn't see beyond the rolling hill behind the barn, she could hear cattle bawling and the high-pitched whistles of the cowboys as they tried to herd the animals back into the fenced enclosure where Grant wintered part of the herd. She grinned when she heard the excited yips of the dogs as they raced to help.

Chilled, she returned inside and made a cup of tea. After selecting one of the cinnamon cookies she'd baked that morning, she went into the front room. She settled onto the couch, kicked off her shoes, and tucked her feet up beneath her skirts. She sipped her tea, ate her cookie, and studied the tree. It really was one of the prettiest she'd ever seen.

Light shining in the window reflected and refracted in the glass balls and crystal icicles hanging on the tree, creating a shimmering rainbow. She relaxed and drew in a deep breath redolent with the fragrance of Christmas. The scent of the tree mingled with the odor of the spices she'd used in her morning baking, and the slight hint of smoke from the wood crackling in the fireplace blended into a comforting aroma.

Cora Lee couldn't explain it, but she felt like this was going to be a special Christmas. One she'd always remember. From the beautiful tree to the welcoming home decorated with garlands and bows, she was surrounded by lovely things and lovely people.

Suddenly tired, she snuggled down into the softness of the couch cushions, pulled a quilt over her legs, and decided a short rest wouldn't hurt anything.

When her eyes drifted shut, she didn't fight sleep as it claimed her. She dreamed of Jace and little boys who looked like him with his dark hair and teasing smile. Would they have all sons? Cora Lee didn't care, just as long as she and Jace were together.

Something cold on her cheek startled her awake. Her eyes popped open and she looked into Jace's face. Only it wasn't his.

Jace would have smiled at her, his eyes soft and inviting. He would have caressed her cheek with the back of his hand, or bent down and kissed her tenderly.

There wasn't a single soft or tender thing about the man looming over her, even if he looked just like Jace. She blinked her eyes and opened them again, but the scowling, bedraggled man wasn't Jace. He stood far too close to her for her liking. It was then she noticed his eyes. They weren't hazel like Jace's, but a deep shade of brown.

"Jude?" she asked, sitting up and swinging her feet over the edge of the couch. She started to draw in a breath and nearly coughed at the stench wafting from him. He looked as though he hadn't bathed in days, possibly weeks. His clothes were filthy and smeared with dried blood. She had no idea if the blood belonged to him or someone else.

Fearful of why he was there and what he intended to do, she tried not to let it show. Instead, she schooled her features into cool indifference as she rose to her feet.

"If it ain't my pretty lil' bride." Jude sneered at her. "You mean to tell me my idiot brother hasn't put a ring on your finger yet?"

"What he has or hasn't done isn't really your concern, is it?" Cora Lee folded the quilt and draped it over the arm of the couch, subtly edging away from this horrid man she had a hard time connecting to the Coleman family. He was nothing like Grant or Jace.

Jude grabbed her arm and spun her around, forcing her to face him. "You're a sassy one, ain't you?" He gave her a long, intense look that made her feel as though she stood before him naked instead of fully clothed. "Maybe I ought to put my claim on you before Jace gets around to it. You ain't half bad to look at, and I like 'em lively."

Cora Lee wrenched her arm away from him and moved back, making sure she was far enough away he couldn't grab her again. "I assume there is a reason you are here. Are you hungry?"

"Starved. Put some food in a basket, and gather up Aunt Mae's doctoring things, then we need to get going."

Cora Lee crossed her arms over her chest and widened her stance. "I'm not leaving with you."

"Yes, you are. Now get busy packing stuff before I have to force you to do it."

She held his gaze, refusing to be intimidated. "No."

One minute Jude was standing across the room glowering at her. The next, he'd jumped over a table, knocking it and one of the side chairs over, and shattering a lamp into broken shards of glass. His hand encircled her neck, squeezing until she grabbed his arm, desperate for him to release her.

"I should have shot you on the train the first time I laid eyes on you. Now listen to me, missy. You get what I told you to like a good girl, and you might live to see another Christmas. If you don't, if you try to outsmart me, or refuse to listen, you'll regret it. Do I make myself clear?"

Unable to nod in agreement, Cora Lee blinked her eyes. Blackness began to edge into her vision causing her to fight back her welling sense of panic.

Jude let her go with a shove. She stumbled back into the dining room table, catching herself before she toppled to the floor, but knocking over two chairs in the process. Gasping, she drew in great lungfuls of air. With a disgusted look at him, she didn't make any move to comply with his wishes. No doubt existed in her mind that Jude was not a man of his word and she'd likely end up dead whether she helped him or not. At least if she remained on the ranch, there was a chance someone might rescue her before it was too late. It was too bad all the hired hands were off rounding up the cattle.

Awareness of who had to be behind the stampede filled her thoughts. She lifted her chin slightly. "You scared the cattle. Caused them to stampede."

Jude grinned, showing tobacco-stained teeth. "Sure did. How else was I gonna keep any of those two-bit numskulls from seeing me haul you outta here?"

It was on the tip of her tongue to set Jude straight on who was lacking intelligence and who was not, with him at the top of the list of idiots, but she managed to keep her thoughts to herself.

"I'm not leaving here with you," Cora Lee said, moving around the table, once again placing herself out of Jude's reach. She continued backing up, hoping she could reach the counter and grab something to defend herself with if he attempted to squeeze the life out of her again.

"You can either leave with me or die right here in the kitchen. Your choice. Either way, get busy filling a basket with food. I'm not the only one who's hungry."

So, he wasn't alone. Cora Lee had a good idea

who was with him. Jace had mentioned robbers had tried and failed to hold up the train he'd driven to Portland, but a few of the outlaws had been shot. She wondered if Jude had an injured outlaw with him, and thus the reason he wanted Mae's basket of medical supplies.

"I'm not doing anything you say. You are nothing but a coward and a bully. It's hard to imagine you being related to Grant and Jace."

Jude pulled a gun from his belt and pointed it at her. "Last time I'm offering to leave you alive."

Cora Lee knew he'd kill her and think nothing of it. He was that sort of cruel, heartless animal. Resigned to doing what he asked, she pulled a basket from a shelf and began to add in a few cookies, a loaf of bread Mae had baked yesterday, half a dozen apples, and what was left of the ham they'd eaten for dinner the previous evening.

"Add more cookies," Jude ordered, waggling the gun toward the cookie jar. She added two big handfuls to the basket, tucked a clean cloth over the top, and slid it down the counter toward Jude.

"Is that sufficient?" she asked in a derisive tone.

"For the moment. I heard you're a good cook. Might have to keep you with us to do our cooking. Beans and hardtack are getting mighty old." Jude took a step toward her. "Where's Aunt Mae's medicinal supplies?"

"I'm not certain," Cora Lee said, which was the truth. Mae had shown her the basket when she'd restocked it after she'd delivered the Garbaldi's baby, but Cora Lee hadn't watched where she'd stored it. "In her room?"

Jude rolled his eyes. "Go look, and don't try anything, or I'll shoot you dead faster than you can blink."

Cora Lee glared at him but walked out of the kitchen, turned into the hall, and headed into Mae's room. She could hear Jude banging around in the kitchen as he searched for it.

While he was occupied, she raced over to the small desk in the corner of Mae's room, scribbled a hasty note, and stuffed it inside her sleeve. She didn't bother to search Mae's room but peeked into the hallway, then dashed into hers, pulling on the wool socks and a pair of boy's britches Mae had given her to wear when she'd gone tree hunting with Grant and Jace. She had a feeling she'd need all the extra warmth she could get if Jude was taking her very far. Quickly yanking on a sweater, she returned to the kitchen just as Jude located the basket on a shelf beneath the sink.

"I got it. Let's go." Jude waggled his gun at her, then pointed to the back door.

"May I at least put on a coat?" Cora Lee asked, marching over to where she'd hung her older wool coat. She slipped it on, wrapped a scarf over her ears and around her neck, then pulled on her boots.

"Why can't women ever just go? You take everlastingly forever to put on a coat!" Jude yelled, then gave her a shove toward the door. "Move!"

Cora Lee walked outside, then looked back to see he'd stepped onto the back porch with only one basket. "You forgot the food."

"Then go grab it. And hurry up about it!" Jude

pointed the gun in her face, looking like he was about to lose what little restraint he owned.

Cora Lee ran inside, grabbed the basket off the counter, let the note fall from her sleeve, and rushed back outside, pulling the door closed behind her.

It was then she noticed two horses tied to the hitching rail near a tree where an old wooden swing hung from a high branch.

"I don't know how to ride," she said over her shoulder as Jude walked behind her. Grant, Jace, and even some of the cowboys on the ranch had been teaching her to ride, but she hadn't had much time for lessons, and with the snow and the approaching holiday, she hadn't been out on a horse for more than two weeks. She knew the rudiments of mounting and staying on, but she didn't feel comfortable riding alone, or without someone to guide and help her.

"Guess you're about to learn," Jude said, taking the basket from her when they reached the horses. He took the reins for the older-looking horse and handed them to her. "Mount up."

Cora Lee looked from him to the stirrup that seemed impossibly high. If he expected her to lift her skirts practically over her head to reach it, he had better think again. She glanced around for a stump or something to use as a step.

Jude must have figured out her dilemma because he draped the baskets from his saddle horn, stormed over to her, grabbed her around the waist, and roughly tossed her into the saddle. Cora Lee grabbed the horn to keep from sailing off the other side. Once she righted herself, she slid her feet into stirrups that were a little too long for her.

With a dark scowl at her, he swung onto his horse, rode back to her, took the reins in his hand, and headed away from the house. They were headed toward the mountain where she'd watched Jace chop the Christmas tree. Was that just yesterday? At the moment, it seemed like a lifetime ago.

She could still hear the ranch hands gathering the cattle in the distance. Jude had sent them scattering in the opposite direction of where they were headed, making sure he could ride in and out unseen.

A hundred questions rushed through her head, but she remained silent, holding onto the saddle horn. Terrified of what Jude and his friends would do to her, Cora Lee finally realized the only thing she could do was pray. If her prayers were answered, Jace would arrive home and find the note in time to help her before it was too late.

Jude rode in the snow that had been packed down by the sleigh runners on their tree-getting expedition. Before he reached the point where they'd stopped the sleigh, he turned and headed up into the trees, threading his way on a path Cora Lee could make out among the sun-dappled shadows cast by the towering conifers.

"Bet Aunt Mae loved the tree you all hauled home yesterday," Jude said, glancing back at her. "You picked a real nice one."

Stunned that he'd spied on them, Cora Lee couldn't think of a response.

Jude looked back at her and chuckled. "I been keeping an eye on things, even if Pa and Jace don't know it. Like I know Pa went with Jace into town today to see Aunt Mae off in Baker City. He does that every year; then he does a little shopping before he heads home." An almost wistful expression settled on his face. "Used to go with him when we were younger. Those were some fun times."

"You grew up in such a nice, loving family, Jude. Why did you turn to a life of debauchery and crime?" Cora Lee kept her tone light and pleasant, as though she'd just asked someone to pass the sugar at an afternoon tea.

Jude glared over his shoulder at her. "Not that it's any of your business, but I'll tell you. My pa always favored Jace. Always. Held him up as an example I should follow. Jace was the thoughtful one, who picked flowers for our cousins or did extra chores for Aunt Mae without being asked. He was the smart one, always getting good grades in school while I hated every living minute of being stuck inside a classroom. Bunch of nonsense they stuff into your head anyway. Every time I'd do something Pa didn't like, he'd sit me down and say, 'Why can't you be more like your brother?' So, I finally decided to be as unlike Jace as I could get."

"I do believe you've succeeded."

Jude looked like he considered riding back and slapping her, so she snapped her mouth shut before she further provoked him. He fell silent as they continued riding up and up deeper into the trees. They were about halfway up the mountain when he changed direction and backtracked for several yards before he started heading east.

How would Jace or Grant possibly find her?

Night was fast approaching, and it would be impossible to follow the tracks in the dark. Feeling sick with worry, she clung to the saddle horn as Jude led the horses around a huge craggy rock that was slippery with snow. Before them, an opening to a cave came into view.

Shocked that there was a cave there and Jude had been hiding in it, she wondered if Jace or Grant knew about it. If so, one of them surely would have come up here looking for Jude.

He led the horses inside and swung off his. She could see three other horses hobbled and eating hay near the entrance. It had to be a sizeable cave if humans and animals shared it.

"Get down," Jude ordered, looping the reins of both horses around a metal ring someone had driven into the rock wall of the cave. He grabbed the baskets from his saddle, then impatiently waited for her to do as he said.

"Does Jace know about this place?" She managed to dismount without tripping on her skirt. Grateful she'd had the foresight to pull on the wool pants, she couldn't imagine how uncomfortable and cold the ride would have been without them as well as the extra clothing she'd hastily donned.

"No, Jace doesn't know about it. I only happened to find it a few years ago. It's been a home away from home." Jude shifted both baskets to one hand, took his gun from his belt with the other, and pointed it at her again. "Move."

"Lead the way," she said, offering him an overly bright, entirely fake smile.

He frowned, then moved in front of her. "Try

and run, and you are dead," he growled over his shoulder as he walked deeper into the cave. The amber glow of a fire provided light up ahead.

The wide entrance narrowed to what seemed more like a hallway before it angled slightly to the left, then opened up into a spacious cavern. Three men sat on stumps near a blazing fire. When Jude appeared with her trailing behind him, they stood and gave her appraising, lascivious looks.

"Hold that thought, fellas. I brought her here to help with Boyd. Don't go getting any ideas," Jude said, motioning for Cora Lee to follow him over to a prone figure shivering on a pile of blankets, all of which looked dirty and smelled even worse. She hid her disgust but wanted to cover her nose to the smell of something putrid that clung to the sick man.

"What's wrong with him?" she asked, looking at the pale, clammy face of the man on the blankets then to Jude.

"He took a bullet a few days ago. Thought it would be fine, but turns out it's not." Jude handed Mae's basket to her. "Fix it."

Cora Lee gaped at him. "I have no medical training. Why didn't you take him into town to see Doctor Holt? He could at least provide proper care."

"Can't risk getting caught," Jude said with a shrug. He handed the basket of food to the outlaw closest to him. "Don't eat all that, Eugene. Boyd needs something, too."

"Sure, boss. Whatever you say." The filthy degenerate grinned, showing a missing front tooth. With stringy hair and skin that appeared to be embedded with grime, Cora Lee couldn't help but question how Jude could prefer the company of these men to his own flesh and blood. Instead of hiding in a cold cave in the mountains, he could be home at the ranch, sitting by the fire beside a beautiful Christmas tree, enjoying a warm, filling meal.

Nothing the man did made sense to her. From what she'd observed and heard from Mae and Grant, they'd done everything they could to help Jude. Mae had told her that when the boys were young, Jace had taken the blame for things Jude had done until they'd finally figured out Jude was the one who should be in trouble. It was as though he wanted to coast through life, doing whatever he pleased, without being troubled by responsibility or consequences.

One day, it was all going to catch up to him. Cora Lee could only hope that day would soon arrive.

Jude pointed to the man on the blankets. "Get busy, missy. He's getting weaker by the minute."

The man's deathly pallor made Cora Lee assume he was beyond saving, but she didn't voice her opinions. She removed her mittens, tucked them into the pocket of her coat, then faced Jude. "Where is he injured?"

"Left side. It bled something awful. I was sure the sheriff was gonna find us just following the crimson trail he left in the snow, but we lost him when we rode through a creek bed." Jude smiled, as though quite proud of his evasive efforts. "It'll take more than a small-town lawman to put the Davis

Gang behind bars."

"And that's who you are? The Davis Gang? Where does that name come from?"

"Thet was the old boss's name, till this 'un decided to take over. Clint Davis rode out one morning and never did come back," Eugene said. "I reckon Jude done set him straight on a few things."

A dark cloud moved across Jude's face. He turned the gun toward Eugene. "Don't you forget what I'm willing to do to have things go my way."

Eugene looked frightened for a moment, then went back to tearing a hunk of bread off the loaf. He wrapped it around a piece of meat before he savagely bit into it, licking the juice from the meat off his fingers. The other men tore into the food with equally barbaric behavior.

Cora Lee thought the animals at the ranch exhibited far better manners.

"Don't just stand there gawking, girl. Do something," Jude ordered.

Cora Lee knelt on the hard rock floor, lifted the blanket away from Boyd's side, and fought the urge to gag. The wound was infected and oozing and held the stench of something decaying. Red streaks ran up and down his body from the wound site. She dropped the blanket and turned away, pressing her face into the shoulder of her coat and taking a deep breath.

She rose and faced Jude. "May I please speak with you a moment, Mr. Coleman?"

Jude started to say something, looked at the dying man on the blanket, then nodded once. He grabbed her arm and propelled her back toward the front of the cave, stopping before they reached the horses. "Well, spit it out, girl. What do you have to say?"

"I'm no expert, but even I can see the wound is infected, and he isn't long for this world. I don't believe even the most skilled doctor could save him at this point."

Jude sighed, then yanked off his hat and ran a hand through his dirty hair. "I sure hate to lose him. Boyd was a good one to have beside you in a fight." He set his hat back on his head, gave Cora Lee a disappointed look, then shoved her toward the back of the cave. "Reckon the best thing to do would be to put him out of his misery."

Appalled at his line of thinking, Cora Lee stopped so abruptly, Jude nearly plowed over her. "Are you insane?" she asked already knowing the answer. "He's not an injured horse or dog. That's a human life you're thinking about ending. You might believe otherwise, but you aren't God. That's not your decision to make."

Jude backhanded her so hard she flew back several feet before she fell to the ground. Blood trickled from a cut on her lip, and her cheek ached, but she refused to be cowed by this madman. With effort, she rose to her feet, fisted her hands on her hips in her best imitation of Mae, and pinned Jude with a fury-filled glare. "You will not shoot that man. You absolutely won't."

With a sneer, Jude lifted the gun as he stalked over to her, holding it in front of her face. "Well, how about I just shoot you instead?"

Chapter Fourteen

"You get everything you needed?" Grant asked as Jace helped him carry their purchases onto one of the Holiday Express passenger cars.

"I think so. I'm sure glad Aunt Mae told us about the girls being fond of dresses from Mrs. Dalton's shop." Jace slid the box he carried beneath a seat, then waited as his dad placed another one next to it.

"I think Anne will also be pleased she mentioned it to R.C." Grant settled onto the seat, and Jace plopped next to him.

Although Jace was supposed to be driving the train, there was a newly trained engineer he'd been working with who'd volunteered to take over duties for the final run of the day. Jace was more than happy to let Tommy do the work. In fact, Tommy would ride in the engine with him on this trip back to Holiday, then be ready to drive the train to Baker City and back again on the day's final round trip.

Early this morning, as they'd ridden in the

sleigh into Holiday, Mae had told him about the shopping excursion she'd made with Cora Lee and Anne. She mentioned both girls had tried on dresses they'd loved but refused to buy. His aunt had gone on to say Cora Lee was careful with her money but not stingy, and that he couldn't find a better bride than if she picked one out for him herself.

"So, the story about all those men in town, including the preacher and Doc, chasing after Cora Lee was for my benefit?" he'd asked, looking from his aunt to his father.

Sheepishly, they'd both nodded.

When they'd reached the livery stable where they'd left the team and sleigh, Mae had spoken to R.C. about Anne's interest in the dress. He'd asked Jace to see if it was still available and if so, to get it, and he'd pay him back.

Jace had been more than happy to pick up the dress for Anne as well as the one Cora Lee liked. Maggie Dalton, the owner of the dress shop, had assured him the gowns wouldn't be the same without new hats. She'd thrown in matching gloves to complete the ensembles, then wrapped the gifts in beautiful foil paper with satin ribbons. Jace had rushed to finish his Christmas shopping, then met his father for an early lunch at their favorite restaurant.

Tommy had come looking for him, and he'd purchased dessert for his fellow engineer. Tommy was three years older than Jace but had less experience. But barring any train robberies or natural disasters, Tommy wouldn't have any problems taking over the afternoon run.

Together, they'd made their way to the depot after Jace had paid the restaurant bill. Grant had dashed back to the mercantile to pick up something he'd forgotten, while Jace made all the arrangements for Tommy to take over as engineer on the final run of the day.

Now, as they sat together in the passenger car, Jace couldn't wait to get home. Back to Cora Lee.

"Is the dress as pretty as Mae said?" his dad asked.

Jace nodded, envisioning the picture Cora Lee would make when she wore it. "It's a beaut, Pops, just like my girl."

"Your girl. I like the sound of that." Grant smiled at him, then elbowed him in the side. "Think it would work as a wedding gown?"

"Maybe," Jace said, then rose from his seat, not wanting to bare his heart to his dad when he still hadn't worked up the courage to tell Cora Lee he loved her. "I'd better get this train ready to roll on down the tracks. Enjoy the ride."

Before his father could comment more about weddings, Jace stepped off the car, jogged to the engine, and climbed on.

The drive back to Holiday was uneventful, other than a herd of elk being close enough to the tracks on either side that Jace could have jumped off the engine onto one. At least none of them were on the tracks. Once, he'd come around a bend and plowed into three elk before the rest of the herd had scattered. He'd hated that it happened, but it was one of the dangers of having train tracks running through the wilderness.

When the train neared the station at Holiday, Jace tooted the whistle, pleased they'd made good time. Admittedly, he might have pushed the engine more than he normally would in his haste to get back to the ranch and Cora Lee.

"Whoo! That was a fine run," the fireman said as he used a coal-smeared bandana to wipe the sweat from his brow before shoving it back in his pocket. "I reckon I won't be seeing you for a few days."

"Nope, Wiley. I'll be back on the twenty-seventh. I hope you have a wonderful Christmas." Jace shook his friend's hand. He pulled a crate with a few paper-wrapped parcels from where he'd stowed it and handed it to Wiley. "Just a little something for Mary and the children."

"That's right kind of you, Jace. Thank you." Wiley took the crate with a grateful nod. "Blessings to you and your family. May this Christmas be your best one yet."

"I'm counting on it," Jace said, grinning at Wiley as he stepped off the engine and turned it over to Tommy.

"Take good care of Hope," he said, tipping his head to the engine. "And Merry Christmas."

"I will, Jace. Your Holiday Hope is safe with me. Merry Christmas to you!" Tommy swung onto the engine with a wave.

Jace hurried to find his father and help him with their purchases; then they made their way to R.C.'s place.

The clang of metal on iron led them through the livery and into the blacksmith shop where R.C.

hammered a red-hot piece of metal on an anvil. He wore a thin shirt with a heavy leather apron over it, and sweat poured off his face. In spite of the chilly temperature, it was exceedingly warm near the forge where R.C. worked.

R.C. happened to glance up and notice their approach. He nodded at them, then gave the horseshoe he was shaping a few more taps before he dipped it into a bucket of water. A loud sizzling sound and a metallic odor filled the air.

"Howdy, there," R.C. said, grinning at them both as he yanked off his gloves. "How was the trip?"

"Great," Grant said. "The ride was as smooth as butter, even when we went through a herd of elk."

"Aren't they something to see?" R.C. asked, looking at the boxes of packages and parcels the two Coleman men carried. He looked around his shop, as though he expected his wife to be spying on them. "Did you find the thing Mae mentioned?" he asked in a whisper.

"Sure did. Mrs. Dalton even wrapped it up." Jace dug the gift out of the big box he carried. "There's a hat and gloves in there, too."

"Great! What do I owe you?" Jace told him the total, then suggested R.C. could just take it off the bill Jace owed for leaving his horse, or sometimes the team, there while he worked.

"You know I don't care if you leave your animals here, Jace."

"If it were anyone else you'd charge a boarding fee, so it's only fair I pay the same." Jace knew

R.C. did well enough with his work that he wasn't hurting for money, but he also knew the man wanted to build a house for his bride so she wouldn't have to continue living in the apartment above the livery.

"Fine, you can pay half the price I'd charge others." R.C. smirked at him. "And that's my final offer."

Grant chuckled and thumped R.C. on the back, then looked to Jace. "You two settle up while I hitch the team to the sleigh. I'm ready to head on home unless you have other errands to see to, son."

"No, Pops. I want to get back to the ranch."

"And Cora Lee," R.C. added, batting his eyelashes at Jace and resting his hands beneath his chin in a pose that made all three of them burst into laughter.

"I thought I heard someone out here," Anne said, stepping into the blacksmith shop with a heavy shawl wrapped around her shoulders.

"Hello, Anne," Jace said, greeting her with a smile. He stepped to the side in front of R.C. so his friend had a chance to hide the Christmas gift he held. "How does this day find you?"

"Happy and well," she said, smiling at him, then at his father. "Hello, Mr. Coleman."

"Grant. You're supposed to call me Grant," his father said.

Anne nodded. "I know, but it just doesn't seem proper," she said in her British accent.

"And she's all about what's proper," R.C. said, kissing his wife's cheek, then frowning at the dirty smear he left on her milky skin.

Anne didn't seem to mind or care as she gazed adoringly at her husband. "I'm not entirely about what's proper. I love you, after all."

R.C. clutched his chest and staggered backward, as though she'd delivered a mortal wound. "Such words cut deep, wife. So deep."

Anne giggled and reached out and took R.C.'s big hand between both of hers. Jace caught the private, tender look that passed between the two of them. He couldn't wait to share something similar with Cora Lee. Perhaps he wouldn't wait until tomorrow to tell her how he felt. Tonight seemed like as good a time as any. If she felt the same and was willing, he hoped they might even wed before the new year. He knew many people married during the holiday season, but he would want Aunt Mae and his cousins present, if possible. Cora Lee might even want to wait until spring and have a grand affair outdoors.

He hoped that wasn't the case. A simple exchange of vows in front of Pastor Ryan was more than sufficient, especially since he couldn't wait for Cora Lee to be his; if she agreed to have him.

"Come on, Pops. Let's head home," Jace said, nudging his father toward the door.

"In a rush, are we?" Anne teased as she and R.C. followed them into the livery. R.C. helped Grant hitch the team.

Jace stowed their purchases in the sleigh, then looked at Anne. "You'll still join us for Christmas Day, won't you?"

"We wouldn't miss it. The invitation is much appreciated." Anne gave him a studying glance.

"When are you going to tell Cora Lee the truth?"

"The truth?" Jace asked, confused.

"That you love her, you ninny." Anne patted his back like he was a clueless child as he gaped at her.

Just how many people knew he cared for Cora Lee?

Anne offered him an indulgent smile. "I'm certain you will find her quite pleased to hear what you have to say, as long as you speak from your heart."

"Is that so?" Jace asked, studying the lovely woman his friend had wed. Not only was she pretty, but she was also smart and kind.

"It is so." Anne stepped back as Grant climbed into the sleigh and Jace slid onto the seat. "Think about what I said, Jace."

"I will. You two take care, and we'll see you tomorrow at the Christmas Eve service."

"Bye!" R.C. and Anne waved as Jace guided the team onto the street.

Before they were more than a few yards on their way, Pastor Ryan waved for them to stop. They'd barely finished speaking to him about coming for Christmas dinner when Doctor Holt flagged them down. It took another thirty minutes of visiting with people they knew before they were finally able to continue on their way.

"R.C. and Anne sure make a nice couple," Grant observed as they glided out of town and headed toward the ranch.

"They do make a fine couple. I'm so grateful R.C. is happy. He deserves it."

"That he does." Grant nodded in agreement, then gave Jace a long glance. "And so do you."

Jace felt his father's hand rest on his shoulder. He turned to look at him. "Thanks, Pops."

"I mean it, Jace. I know life hasn't been easy for you, especially with your brother being so ... well, so himself, but you deserve to know true happiness. Unless I'm wildly mistaken, I think you'll find it with Cora Lee."

"If she loves me even half as much as I love her, I think we have a chance at being incredibly happy together." Jace sighed. "You don't think she'll be like my mother, do you?"

Grant scoffed, appearing appalled. "Cora Lee? That sweet girl? Never. She is nothing like your mother. Aria was always conceited and selfish and manipulative. If I hadn't been so blinded by her beauty, I might have noticed it before I married her. But I want you to know something, son."

"What's that?" Jace asked, glancing at his father, then back at the road.

"If I had to do it over again, I'd still marry Aria."

Jace stared at his father, baffled by his comment. "Why in the world would you put yourself through all that heartache and pain a second time?"

"Because every bit of it was worth getting you and your brother." Grant settled an arm around his shoulder and gave it a squeeze.

Warmed by his father's words and affection, he nodded in appreciation to Grant. "Thank you, Pops. I couldn't imagine having any better father than you."

"Oh, I think there are quite a few who could have done a better job raising you boys. I can't help but think if I'd done something different, perhaps your brother would be different."

Jace shook his head. "You raised us the same, Pops. Jude made his choices, and I made mine. It's not your fault he took the path he's on."

"Maybe, maybe not. Nevertheless, I fear that path is leading somewhere that won't end well. Not at all."

A sigh rolled out of Jace. "I know. I worry about him too. As Aunt Mae would say, all we can do is lift him up in prayer and leave it at that."

"Your aunt is a wise one, but don't tell her I said that."

Jace grinned. "I won't."

Although he couldn't explain it, a pressing feeling settled over him to get home and make sure Cora Lee was safe. The reasonable side of his brain knew nothing would happen to her at the house, especially with the ranch hands all there, but dread unfurled inside him until he found it hard to breathe.

When he clucked to the team and urged them to go faster, his father didn't question him. He appeared as concerned as Jace suddenly felt.

As soon as they reached the house, Jace handed the reins to his father and jumped off the sleigh before it came to a full stop. He raced up the front steps and charged into the house.

Upturned furniture, a broken lamp, and Cora Lee's shoes left by the couch did nothing to alleviate his fears.

"Cora Lee!" he called, but the house was silent. "Cora Lee!"

His father rushed in behind him. "Oh, no," he said as he took in the upheaval.

"I'll check in her and Mae's rooms," Jace said while his father headed down the other hallway. It took only a minute for them to return to the front room, growing more concerned by the minute.

"Maybe she's in the outhouse," Grant suggested as they met in the kitchen. The smell of roasting meat filled the house with a delicious scent, so Cora Lee couldn't have been gone that long. Jace started toward the back door and noticed something on the floor.

He picked up the wrinkled piece of paper and carefully smoothed it. After reading the few scribbled words, he slammed his fist onto the counter, making dishes clatter.

"What is it?" Grant asked, taking the paper from him and reading it aloud.

Jude taking me, food, and medicine with him.

"She's a smart girl," Grant said, pointing to the time she'd written on the note. According to it, Jude had taken her about an hour ago. "Do you think he's hurt?"

Jace shook his head. "No. I'd know if that was the case. Besides, if he was the one who needed medicine, he would still be here. I have a feeling it has something to do with the train robbers who were shot the other day. I would bet my last penny that Jude was there when they tried to hold up the train to Portland. One of his cronies is probably injured badly and needs help."

"Most likely, but I don't like the idea of your brother taking Cora Lee with him, especially around any of his friends. They are a rough bunch."

"I don't like it either, Pops!" Jace shouted, angry at his brother and lashing out for all the times Jude had done something stupid or hurtful. "This is Jude. This is what he does."

Grant pulled Jace into a fatherly hug, then quickly let him go. "Let's go find him and get Cora Lee back. I can't think he'd have taken her far."

"We should ask some of the boys to help search," Jace said. "They can check the line shacks and see if Jude's holed up in one of them. There's the old falling-down cabin in the woods where we used to play. And there's also a cave Jude sometimes hides in that he thinks no one knows about."

"Then that's probably where he is. You know how to get to the cave?"

Jace nodded. "I do. If you want to pull on some warmer clothes, I'll go tell Nolan and the others what's happening and saddle the horses."

"I'll gather a change of clothes for you." Grant hurried toward his room while Jace raced outside. He drove the sleigh to the barn, yelling for someone to help him, but no one appeared. That's when he heard the sound of the cows bawling and cowboys hollering in the distance. Something must have happened with the herd.

Whatever the problem, he had no time to worry about it now. Jace hurriedly unhitched the team and led them into their stalls in the barn, saddled Jericho and his dad's favorite horse, then led them back to the house.

"Go change. I left a cup of coffee on the counter for you. Drink it to warm up your insides; then we'll be on the way," Grant said as he hurried down the steps. He looked toward the sound of the cattle, then back at Jace.

"What's going on?"

"I don't know, but I'd wager Jude had something to do with it." Jace strode into the house, changed out of his engineer clothes into his ranch clothes, added extra socks, and then fastened on his gun belt. He filled his pockets with extra cartridges, picked up his rifle, and stopped only long enough to hastily swallow the cup of coffee that had cooled enough it didn't burn his tongue.

"Please, Lord, let her be all right," he muttered before he stormed outside, shoved the rifle into the scabbard on his saddle, and swung onto Jericho's back.

His father rode around the side of the house, motioning for him to follow. "Two horses went off in this direction. Most likely Jude. Looks like he followed the tracks we made with the sleigh when we went to get the tree."

"That's not all that far from the cave," Jace said, urging Jericho into a run. Rather than follow where the tracks left the trail made by the sleigh, Jace followed the base of the mountain around a fallen cottonwood tree near the creek.

"Do you see anything?" his dad asked in a quiet voice.

"Not yet. The cave is about a quarter-mile from here. If that's where he took her and others are there, things could be bad for Cora Lee. I need to know what you're willing to do to help her, Pops." Jace gave his father an earnest, questioning look.

"If it comes down to me disabling Jude or even shooting him to save her, I'll do it," Grant said in a hard, unyielding tone. "Jude's made his choices and it's far past time for him to face the consequences. The important thing is rescuing Cora Lee."

Jace nodded once, then glanced at the sky. The sun was about to sink. If they waited any longer, they'd be riding into a potential ambush in the dark. With caution, but mindful of the need for urgency, they rode to the cave. When they reached it, Jace dismounted and motioned for his dad to tie the horses to a tree far enough away from the entrance they wouldn't be seen.

"I had no idea this was here," Grant said in a hushed voice. "How long have you known about it?"

"Since we moved here," Jace whispered. "A boy needs a good hiding spot, you know."

In spite of the circumstances, his father grinned at him, then motioned for him to lead the way. On silent feet, they made their way toward the craggy rocks, then edged around them to the cave opening.

A dim amber glow at the back of the large open room in the front of the cave looked like it might come from a fire. He counted five horses in the rapidly dimming afternoon light. He tipped his head back in the way they'd come. When they were several feet away from the cave, he turned to his father.

"Five horses and only one of them belongs to Jude. I'm going to assume there are five men in there, one or more possibly injured. We need to come up with a plan."

"Agreed," his father said, rubbing a hand over his jaw. "Maybe we could draw one or two out at a time, then go in and get Cora Lee."

"We could hide in the shadows, behind the horses, make a little noise, and see who comes out to check on them."

Grant nodded. "Let's do it."

Together, they returned to the cave opening. They'd just eased inside when voices carried back to them.

Jace froze as he heard Jude speak.

"Well, spit it out, girl. What do you have to say?" his brother asked in his nasally, whiny voice.

"I'm no expert," Cora Lee said, "but even I can see the wound is infected and he isn't long for this world. I don't believe even the most skilled doctor could save him at this point."

Jude was silent a moment before he spoke again. "I sure hate to lose him. Boyd was a good one to have beside you in a fight."

The voices grew muffled, and Jace strained to hear what was said, but couldn't. He heard shuffling feet; then what sounded like someone being struck, and Cora Lee cried out. Infuriated, Jace vowed if Jude hurt one hair on her golden head, he was going to make him pay for it, and pay dearly.

Before he could take a step forward, a hand settled on his shoulder. He glanced back to see the county sheriff, Bert Goodwin, as well as Holiday's marshal, Dillon Durant.

Stunned by their sudden appearance, Jace pointed outside. He and his father followed the men out to where they'd left their horses.

"What are you doing here?" Grant asked, shaking hands with both men.

"The sheriff followed the Davis Gang up into the mountains before he lost their trail, but one of the men he arrested off the train the other day said they sometimes hide in a cave with Jude," Marshal Durant said.

"Which led me to Holiday to see if Dillon knew Jude's whereabouts, or how to find the cave," the sheriff said. "We were almost to your house when we saw you two riding away, following what appeared to be tracks. Do you know if Jude's in there with the gang?"

"I just heard Jude talking. He kidnapped the woman I intend to marry. From what was said, it sounds like one of the gang members is hurt badly," Jace said, grateful for extra help but eager to get to Cora Lee. He was sure she was the one who had cried out, and he was concerned Jude had hurt her. "There are five horses in the cave opening, so we assumed there are probably five men."

"Benny Boudry said there are anywhere from six to ten in their gang, depending on what and where they are planning a robbery. I arrested him and another yahoo the other day and picked up three more members of the gang yesterday in Pendleton. If there are five of them in there, then that should be all of the gang." The sheriff toyed with the end of his mustache. "I don't want to run in there with guns blazing and risk the woman getting hurt. Did you two have a plan?" He looked from Jace to Grant.

"We were going to see if we could draw out a couple of them and get them out of the way," Jace said.

The sheriff nodded. "That will work. Using the horses to hide behind?"

Jace nodded. "That was my plan."

"Then let's get to it," the sheriff started back into the cave. He and Grant took one side of the cave, while Jace and Dillon crept along the other. When they were hidden deep in the shadows behind the horses, Dillon reached out and slapped the flank of the horse nearest him.

It whinnied and shied away, making enough racket that it echoed off the rock walls of the cave.

They didn't have to wait more than a minute before one of the outlaws appeared. Jace recognized him as one of Jude's cohorts, a halfwit named Eugene. He walked over to the horse and looked around. Before Jace could move, the marshal slipped behind Eugene and conked him over the head with the butt of his pistol.

He dragged Eugene's limp body into the shadows. After cuffing his hands, Jace stuffed a dirty bandana he pulled from Eugene's pocket into the man's mouth, taking a bit more satisfaction in the task than he probably should have. Dillon tied Eugene's feet together with a length of rope he pulled from his pocket.

They waited a few moments, and another gang

member appeared. "Eugene! Get your ugly ol' hide back in here. Jude is makin' us flip for who has to shoot Boyd and the girl." He looked around as he approached the horses. "Eugene?"

"He's not here," the sheriff said, stepping from behind a horse and plowing his fist in the outlaw's face before he could shout a warning. Grant supplied a rag to stuff in the outlaw's mouth, while the marshal cuffed him, and the sheriff tied his hands to his feet behind him, leaving him on his belly, trussed up like a turkey.

Assured the two outlaws couldn't get away or interfere, Sheriff Goodwin and Dillon moved deeper into the cave with Jace and Grant behind them. They went through what Jace always thought of as a hallway, then stood in the shadows at the entrance to another large open space.

A fire burned brightly in the center of the room. Cora Lee knelt next to a pallet on the floor where another of Jude's good friends looked like he was only a breath or two away from knocking at death's door. Jude paced back and forth by the fire while a man Jace recognized as someone Jude called Joe sat on the other side of the flames, eating an apple like he didn't have a care in the world.

The sheriff made a few hand motions that Jace took to mean the sheriff would deal with Joe. That meant the rest of them had to be ready to rush in and get Cora Lee to safety before Jude started firing the gun he held in his hand.

Truthfully, Jace had never seen such a wild, crazed look on his brother's face or unsettling gleam in his eyes. He looked nothing like the playmate he remembered from his childhood years. This man was hard and calculating—one who was capable of doing anything to get what he wanted.

Guilt swamped him, making him wish he'd made a point to stop Jude a long time ago instead of ignoring the changes in him. Changes he now realized were deadly.

The sheriff slunk through the shadows until he was behind Joe; then he leaped forward, knocking Joe off the stump where he sat and into the fire.

Joe howled in pain and scrambled up, but the sheriff plowed into him, knocking him off his feet.

While Sheriff Goodwin wrestled with Joe, Jace ran into the cave.

Jude's mouth hung open in surprise, watching the sheriff as though he couldn't grasp the fact that his days as an outlaw were at an end.

While Jude was distracted, Jace dodged around his brother, grabbed a startled Cora Lee, and shoved her behind him.

"Jace," she whispered, putting a world of emotion into the way she said his name. He could feel her trembling as she leaned against his back. "You came."

"I couldn't let anything happen to my best girl," he said, giving her a glance over his shoulder before turning back to face his brother.

The marshal stood on one side of Jude, while his father stood on the other.

"Surrender, son, before anyone else gets hurt," Grant said, taking a step closer to Jude.

"No! I won't do it, Pa, and no one can make me!" Jude shouted. He lifted his gun and aimed it at

Jace. "I should have known you'd show up and ruin everything, just like you always do; like you always have."

Incredulous, Jace wished he could vent his anger and frustration on his brother, like they used to do with fists when they were boys. "I haven't done anything, Jude, except keep you from hurting anyone else. Your friend here needs help."

"Boyd's too far gone to save. Be a favor to him if I just put a bullet in his head." Jude waved his gun toward the sick man. In a silver-quick motion, he cocked the hammer. Grant grabbed his arm as he pulled the trigger and the shot went off course, hitting Joe in the arm.

The outlaw howled in pain, until the sheriff stuffed a bandana in his mouth.

The marshal yanked the gun away from Jude; then Grant grabbed him from behind, locking his arms around his son, keeping him from moving. Dillon grabbed another length of rope from his pocket and tied Jude's wrists before Grant loosened his hold.

Jude vigorously shook his head back and forth, expelling a noise similar to that of a wounded animal.

Jace glanced at his father to make sure his brother was secure and wouldn't cause more harm before he pulled Cora Lee into his arms, holding her close, sheltering her from the scene behind them.

"Cora Lee. Oh, Cora Lee. Are you well? Did he hurt you?" he asked, holding her tenderly as he pressed kisses to her temple and cheeks.

"I'm fine, Jace." She clung to him, and he felt a

shudder rack through her.

"I'd rather die than rot in prison! You can't make me go!" Jude yelled, yanking at the rope binding his wrists.

"You made your choices, son," Grant said solemnly.

"And I'll make this one!" Jude screamed.

"No! No, Jude!" Grant shouted. As though everything happened at a slower pace, Jace watched his brother yank the pistol out of his father's hand and aim it his way. He heard Cora Lee scream as pain exploded in his head. The last thing he remembered was crumpling to the ground.

Jace awoke to a dull thumping in his head and a mouth that tasted like he'd stuffed it full of rancid cotton. He licked his dry lips and sighed, wondering why he felt so tired and why he couldn't get his eyes to open.

The edge of a glass touched his mouth, and he greedily drank the cool water.

Fingers, delicate and light, stroked through his hair, and he drew in a breath, inhaling Cora Lee's soft fragrance. "Cora Lee," he whispered.

"I'm here, Jace. Right here. Just rest. Everything is fine. You just rest."

Jace relaxed and let sleep claim him again. The next time he awakened, streams of light snuck around the edges of the drapes. He looked around a room he didn't recognize, wondering where he could be. A noise next to him drew his gaze to the chair where Cora Lee slept. Her hair was half falling in her face, her clothes were dirty, and her lip sported a bruise with a cut, but he thought she looked wonderful.

The ordeal of the previous afternoon came back to him. Jude in the cave. Gunshots. Cora Lee screaming. Jace reached up and touched a bandage wrapped around his head. He wasn't sure what happened, but it seemed like Jude had shot at him. Maybe his brother had better aim than he used to.

"You're awake," Cora Lee said, her voice sounding thick with emotion. "How do you feel?"

"Like something hit me in the head." He forced himself to smile at her. "Are you well?"

She nodded, tears welling in her eyes. She moved from the chair to gingerly sit beside him on the bed. She took his hand in hers and held it to her cheek. "I'm so glad you're fine, Jace. Does your head hurt terribly bad?"

"Just a dull ache." He tried to sit up, winced, and reclined back against his pillows. "What day is it?"

"Christmas Eve. We're at Doctor Holt's office."

At least he hadn't missed Christmas. "What happened?"

"Jude took exception to you and the others spoiling his plans. He tried to shoot you, but between your father grabbing his arm and the marshal knocking him to the ground, the bullet grazed the side of your head. We're so fortunate it didn't do lasting damage."

Or kill him, Jace thought.

"Is Pops unhurt? The others?" he asked

"Grant is well. The marshal had a few bumps and bruises from fighting Jude all the way down the mountain, and the sheriff had a few as well. Your brother and the others have been taken to the jail in La Grande, and a U.S. Marshal will take them to Portland from there. Since they have committed crimes in multiple counties and two states, they'll have a trial there next month."

Jace tried to grasp everything she said, but his head felt fuzzy, so he focused on what he could. Jude was on his way to prison. Everyone would be fine. "What about Boyd? Did he make it?"

"Sadly, no. He passed before they could get him out of the cave."

"That's too bad," Jace said, feeling sorry for a man who died in such a cold, lonesome place in the midst of turmoil.

Jace stared at Cora Lee, assuring himself she was unharmed, other than the damage to her lip. "I had something I wanted to tell you last night, something I wanted to ask you. Now doesn't seem like the most ideal time, but it can't wait."

He made himself sit up, ignoring the wave of dizziness that accompanied his movement. It took a moment before he convinced himself he wouldn't be ill. Grateful for her help, he took a few sips of water from the glass Cora Lee held for him, then leaned back after she'd adjusted his pillows to support him.

"Surely it can wait, Jace. You need to rest."

"No. I need to do this now." He waited until she resumed her seat on the narrow mattress, facing him, then took one of her hands in his. He brought it to his mouth and kissed the backs of her fingers.

When he lifted his gaze to hers, he saw the

answers to the questions he had yet to ask, and it gave him the encouragement he needed to speak from his heart.

"Cora Lee Schuster, you arrived here in Holiday not even two months ago, expecting to marry a man you never met. I feel like God put you at Elk Creek Ranch for a reason, and it wasn't to marry my horrible brother or to be a hired girl for Mae. He brought us together so we'd fall in love. And I have, Cora Lee. I've fallen for you so completely, so deeply, I can't picture any part of my future without you in it. I love you today with my whole heart. And I'll love you fifty years from now. If you feel the same, would you consider becoming my wife and spending all your tomorrows with me?"

Tears welled in her beautiful blue eyes as she nodded, then leaned forward until she could give him a gentle hug. It used what strength he had to return the embrace and kiss her cheek.

She pulled back but placed a hand on his whiskered chin, lightly brushing her thumb over his bottom lip. Her smile held such warmth, he felt like someone had poured sunshine into his soul.

"I love you, Jace. I have from the first day I met you, and I will until I draw my last breath. It would be a great honor and a blessing to be your wife. Thank you for asking me. Thank you for rescuing me. And most of all, thank you for loving me."

"I love you so much, Cora Lee. If Jude had hurt you, if he'd …"

Her lips on his silenced him, and he decided

planning their future was much more enjoyable than dwelling on the worries of the past.

He returned her kiss, praying they'd have many joyful years ahead of them, years full of laughter, love, and hope.

Chapter Fifteen

New Year's Day, 1885

"You are beautiful," Mae said as she fussed with the lace on Cora Lee's wedding dress.

Cora Lee still couldn't quite believe the glorious gown at Maggie Dalton's shop that she'd so adored was now hers. Jace had given it to her Christmas morning and suggested it might make a nice thing to wear on their wedding day.

He'd been too weak to attend Christmas Eve services but refused to spend Christmas Day in town at the doctor's office. Grant had bundled him up like a baby, in spite of Jace's vehement protests, and brought him home to Elk Creek in the sleigh.

At Jace's insistence, they'd gone ahead with their Christmas dinner as planned. The doctor had been there most of the day to make sure Jace was healing well, and Cora Lee had heard the man tell Jace how fortunate he was the bullet had barely done more than break the skin along his temple.

In spite of all that had transpired with Jude, the

house had rung with happy laughter on Christmas Day. It was then Anne had asked when Jace and Cora Lee planned to wed. Cora Lee had looked at Jace and cheekily replied, "When he's gained his strength back. It wouldn't do for a bride to be forced to carry the groom down the aisle."

Everyone had laughed, but Jace, appearing quite indignant, had given Cora Lee a heated look. "You choose the day, and I'll be ready."

"New Year's Day!" she'd said without a moment of hesitation. Doctor Holt had told her Jace would be fine in a few days, and the thought of being his wife sooner rather than later had made her eager to set their wedding date.

Grant had sent a telegram to Mae, and she'd arrived the previous afternoon with all three of her daughters in tow.

Cora Lee had been delighted to meet them all. She'd felt an immediate kinship with the sweet women who reminded her so much of their mother.

Now, as they gathered around her, making sure every hair was in place, she felt a great wave of love for them all.

"I'm so glad to have all four of you here," she said, smiling at each of them in turn.

"We're thrilled to be here, Cora Lee," Sarah said, kissing her cheek. "Mama said you were perfect for Jace, and she's right. I think the two of you will have many happy years together."

"And we're so happy you'll be part of our family," Flo said, giving her a hug and kissing both of her cheeks.

"But we'd better all leave her be and let Uncle

Grant walk her down the aisle. I'm sure Jace is most anxious for his bride to appear. It wouldn't do to keep him waiting, at least not too long," Em said, grinning as she slipped on her coat and opened the door.

Anne had invited Cora Lee to change into her wedding gown at the home she and R.C. shared above the livery. Although the space was small, it was cozy and warm and full to the rafters with happiness and love.

After Mae and her daughters left to go to the church, Anne gave Cora Lee a long hug. "I'm so happy for you, my friend. May you and Jace always be blessed with love and never lose hope in each other or the future."

"Thank you, Anne," Cora Lee said, dabbing at her eyes with a handkerchief she drew from the sleeve of her exquisite gown. "You look so beautiful in your dress."

"Thank you." Anne smiled and brushed a hand down the skirt of the gown R.C. had given her for Christmas. "I was shocked when I opened it but so happily surprised. It's the finest gown I've ever owned. However, you look breathtaking in that dress, as every bride should."

Cora Lee gripped her friend's hands with hers. "It's all so ... exhilarating and exciting."

"It is. Come on. It's time to head over to the church. Jace has probably worn a hole in the floor, pacing around, waiting for your arrival. My husband might have to tie him to the pulpit to get him to stand still."

A giggle rolled out of Cora Lee, and soon the

two of them were laughing as they made their way down the apartment steps and headed to the church, walking arm in arm.

Grant waited for them outside. He bent over and kissed Cora Lee's cheek. "Welcome to the family, Cora Lee. I'm so proud to call you my daughter. I hope you'll think about calling me Dad or Pops."

"I'd like that, Pops. Thank you. And thank you for making me feel so much a part of the family from the moment I first arrived in Holiday."

"Well, you are, honey, and you have been since the day the two of you stepped off the train," he said, settling her arm on his, then guiding her up the steps to the church door.

Mae lingered there and handed Cora Lee a bouquet of hothouse roses that had come in on the train.

"Jace ordered these but wasn't sure they'd get here in time." Mae gave her one more hug, then disappeared inside.

Soon piano music filtered out to them, and Grant smiled down at her. "Ready?" he asked.

"Yes," she said, grinning at him as they walked inside the church and down the aisle.

Cora Lee felt as if the rest of the world faded away when her gaze connected with Jace's. He stood at the front of the church next to Pastor Ryan and R.C. in a new suit with a starched collar and blue tie, the same color as her eyes. He looked so handsome she could hardly believe she was about to become his bride.

She glanced down and saw he wore the boots

she'd made him for Christmas. Jace had been so proud of them, he'd immediately put them on and had to show them to everyone who'd come to the house on Christmas Day.

When she lifted her eyes to connect with his again, love shimmered in their depths.

What a wondrous thing it was to love and be loved so freely and completely. It was far better than she'd imagined and far more than she'd dared hope.

Cora Lee had left Cincinnati afraid yet determined to make the best of whatever the future might bring. She'd never allowed herself to dream it would include falling in love with a handsome stranger who'd welcomed her not only into his home but into his heart.

"You are glorious," Jace whispered when Grant placed her hand in his.

She beamed at Jace and smiled at his father when he kissed her cheek, then took his place beside Mae in the front row.

Pastor Ryan cleared his throat and began the ceremony. Cora Lee spoke at the proper times and blinked away tears during their vows. When Jace slid a beautiful gold ring on her finger, one teardrop rolled down her cheek. A tear of sheer happiness.

The moment the preacher proclaimed them to be husband and wife, Jace pulled her into his arms and kissed her with passion tempered by promises.

Together, they turned and greeted the congregation that had filled the church. They'd just started down the aisle when a train whistle sounded outside.

Jace swept her into his arms with a laugh, then carried her down the aisle and out the door.

"Goodbye," Cora Lee said over Jace's shoulder as he marched from the church toward the depot, where their luggage was already being loaded on the train. She tossed her bouquet and watched as a shy young woman caught it and buried her nose in the blossoms.

"Be good to her, son, or you'll answer to me," Grant called after them.

"You can lecture me when we get home," Jace hollered, unable to hold back a grin. He carried her up the platform steps and onto the train, then took a seat, settling her across his lap.

She glanced around the car, expecting to see other occupants, but it was empty. "Jace, I should …"

"Stay right where you are," he said, kissing her soundly before he leaned back. "I made arrangements for this car to remain empty on the way to Baker City, unless there isn't another available seat on the entire train, including the caboose."

"You mean we don't have to share with anyone?" she asked, relaxing into the strength of his solid chest.

"No one. Just you and me, my adorable wife." He leaned back and studied her face for a long moment, then released a contented sigh. "You are everything I never knew I wanted or needed, Cora Lee. Thank you for marrying me today."

"It's I who should be thanking you, Jace. You brought me to Holiday on Hope, and together we'll walk into our future with hope. Hope and love, and more happiness and blessings than we can imagine. I'm so grateful for you, for the promise of a lifetime spent together. I hope you know how much I love you."

"I do, my beautiful, Cora Lee. And I love you," Jace whispered, bracketing her face as he kissed her breathless. "Forevermore, I love only you."

Wasn't it wonderful to watch Jace and Cora Lee fall in love?
I was rooting for them from the start!
Keep reading for an excerpt from
Holiday Heart,
the second book in the Holiday Express series!

Apple Kuchen

In the story, Jace and Grant both love sweets. This apple kuchen is something Cora Lee would have made that they both enjoyed. Happy baking!

Apple Kuchen

Cake
1 cup flour
2 tablespoons sugar
1/4 teaspoon salt
1/2 cup butter, softened

Blend together with a fork, or pastry blender, until crumbly and well mixed. Pat into a greased 9" x 9" or 8" x 8" square pan. Set aside.

Filling
4 cups apples, peeled and sliced (Granny Smith works great)
1/2 cup sugar
1 teaspoon cinnamon

Mix apples with sugar and cinnamon. Layer over cake batter.

Topping
1/3 cup flour
1/2 cup sugar
1/4 cup butter, softened
1 teaspoon cinnamon

Use a fork to combine. Sprinkle on top of apples.

Preheat oven to 350 degrees.

Bake for 45-50 minutes, until edges are lightly browned. Serve with lightly sweetened whipped cream or ice cream. Refrigerate leftovers – if you have any!

Author's Note

Sometimes, the idea for a story arrives so unexpectedly, it almost feels like magic or a special gift.

Back in the winter of 2019, Captain Cavedweller and I were driving through Nevada and stopped in the town of Ely. On a whim, we decided to check out the Nevada Northern Railway Museum.

(If you're a fan of the television show "The Big Bang Theory," the museum was mentioned in an episode where Sheldon heads to Nevada for a "Be the Engineer" experience – which is really a thing!)

The day offered brilliant blue skies and cold temps that went with all the snow on the ground, but it was perfect for exploring.

The museum is a national historic landmark, but it's also an operating historical railroad. The brochure offered in the gift shop says: "It's gritty. It's dirty. It smells of coal smoke, creosote, and sweat ..." They aren't exaggerating.

The complex consists of a full-service rail yard encompassing 56 acres with 63 buildings, shops, and structures that served the historic copper mining region of Central Nevada for more than a century. Original railway locomotives, rolling stock, track, a passenger station that includes three steam locomotives (two that are operational), six diesel locomotives, and more than 60 pieces of historic equipment are kept there.

The museum is such a neat place to visit

because you can actually walk into the engine house and watch the mechanics working on train repairs. The morning we wandered in, we'd only been in the building a minute or two when a guy popped up in the smokestack. It's just so interesting and fun to get to see everything up close and firsthand.

There were also a bunch of trains on display. Some of them you could even climb in. One of my favorites made me think of the train on the "The Polar Express."

In 1910, the railroad needed a new locomotive to pull the passenger train on a daily round-trip from Ely to Cobre, hauling passengers, mail, and express shipments. Number 40 was purchased from the Baldwin Locomotive Works for a cost of $13,139. The train entered scheduled service with a speed of 40 miles per hour pulling a railway post office/baggage car and a first-class coach, both of which are still in service at the museum. When the locomotive was no longer needed after World War II, #40 was put on the list to be scrapped. Because the crews loved the engine, it mysteriously disappeared whenever someone in authority came looking for it. Because of the ghost-like movements of the engine, it became known as "The Ghost Train." Thanks to the efforts of the crews, the train survived and still operates today, pulling passengers along the track. This train happens to be the inspiration behind the steam engine Hope featured in this series.

In addition to seeing the locomotives, there were several displays with interesting historical items and information, like a velocipede used to check the track. It looks a lot like a bicycle but instead of rubber tires, it has wheels that fit on a train track. The rider operates it by pushing and pulling the handles while pushing on the pedals. That velocipede is what inspired the scene where Jace rides one to Holiday. I think it would have taken a great deal of strength and endurance to push that thing along the tracks!

You can see some of the photos I took on my blog, or visit the Nevada Northern Railway Museum for more details about their amazing property.

We'd only been in the museum a few minutes when the idea for a mail-order bride story started popping around in my head. What if there was a bride, and she was riding on a brand-new steam engine heading to some remote location? And what if the train was robbed? And what if ...

See how things work in my weird mind?

By the time we finally left the museum a few hours later, the possible mail-order bride story had morphed into a multi-generational series all centered around a steam engine that I decided to name Hope.

And since we were in Nevada with nothing but miles and miles of open road ahead of us, Captain Cavedweller and I had plenty of time for brainstorming and taking notes. In fact, I was the one driving and had to decipher his chicken-scratch penmanship when we got home, but I love that we spent that time together and I love that this series is the result of the trip and the ideas we tossed around in the pickup cab that day.

Welcome to the Holiday Express sweet romance series!

Truly, I adored every bit of writing the four books in this series, and I hope you'll enjoy reading them.

Holiday Hope is the first book and introduces not only the Coleman family, but also the town of Holiday, and each story includes a special visit with a jolly old man named Nick!

Admittedly, I don't know much about trains, but I was fortunate to find some wonderful resource books. One was a reproduction edition of *The Railroad Car Builder's Pictorial Dictionary* by Matthias N. Forney, originally published by the Railroad Gazette back in 1879. The book includes page after page of engravings that show everything from baggage carts and wagons, to the screws and latches used to hold windows shut on passenger cars. A handy "car-building" dictionary also provided helpful terms.

Another find that proved useful was something I happened across in an antique store. Published by Time-Life Books, *The Railroaders* is part of The Old West series of twenty-six books released between 1973 and 1980. Each book includes a variety of illustrations, photographs, and details about the fundamental founding of the American West through a specific topic, such as railroads, cowboys, gamblers, and miners.

The Railroaders offered a wealth of information from what it was like to travel first class or be stuck riding in an immigrant coach. It painted detailed pictures of the opulent Pullman cars and offered some humorous recounting of passengers being tossed from their berths. One woman recalled awakening in her berth to find her neighbor's feet invading her space.

Other tidbits of research mentioned the excitement of passengers when they stopped and a farmer and his wife boarded the train to sell fresh doughnuts. There really were some stops along the way that made prairie dog stew (yuck!).

I greatly enjoyed learning about the men who made the trains roll down the tracks, from the ringmaster (train coordinator or yardmaster) to the shacks (brakemen), to the captain (conductor), to the hogger (the engineer).

Working on the railroad regardless of the job was dangerous. There are many stories of people losing fingers (or their lives) as they hooked or unhooked cars from the train.

I'm not sure which job would have been the worst, but I think that of the brakeman in the winter would have been right up at the top. Back when they used hand brakes that were operated from on top of the cars, the brakemen were out there in freezing temperatures, jumping from one icy car to the next to set the brakes.

In case you are wondering, the engineer and fireman did sometimes cook their meals in the firebox on a flat shovel.

When I was researching historical details from 1884, I happened upon an article in an old newspaper from the area that reported an enormous apple tree had produced a bumper crop of thirty-eight bushels of apples. As Cora Lee said, that's a lot of apple cake!

Oh, I have to share a little about the scene where Cora Lee is helping Mae prepare for the Thanksgiving holiday and watched in wonder as the table expanded with the addition of leaves. After I wrote that, I backtracked because I wasn't sure when table leaves were invented. Turns out, the first table leaf was developed in the 1500s in the form of a drop leaf, or draw leaf table. By the 1700s, Georgian pedestal tables introduced a free-standing leaf inserted between the ends of the pedestal. By the mid-1800s, the modern method of adding a leaf using a sliding rail was developed.

One other historical tidbit I want to share is about the Washington Monument. I stumbled across an article from 1884 that reported the Washington Monument was nearing completion after fifty years. Honestly, I had no idea it had taken that long to build!

If, like me, you don't know the history of the monument, the idea for a monument to honor George Washington was kicked around before he even became president. In 1783, the Continental Congress voted to build a statue of Washington. Once Washington became president, he discarded ideas for a monument since funds were tight and he thought there were better uses of federal funds. After he passed away, Congress again brought up the idea of a monument, but nothing came of it.

Finally, in the 1830s, a group of Washington residents banded together and formed the Washington National Monument Society to raise private funds for the project. The group, headed by

Chief Justice John Marshall, held a design competition. The winning architect was Robert Mills, whose credits include the U.S. Treasury Building and the U.S. Patent Office, currently home to the National Portrait Gallery and the Smithsonian American Art Museum.

Mills' design called for a temple-like building with thirty stone columns and statues of Revolutionary War heroes. The plan was for a statue of Washington driving a chariot to reside above the main entrance with a 600-foot-tall Egyptian obelisk rising from the center of the building.

The monument's cornerstone (embedded with a box that held items such as a portrait of George Washington, newspapers of the day, U.S. coins, and a copy of the Constitution) was placed in a ceremony attended by thousands of people. Construction began, but in 1854, with the structure only 150 feet high, funds ran low, and work stopped. An activities group called the Know Nothings became angry Pope Pius IX had donated a block of stone from the ancient Roman Temple of Concord for the monument. They confiscated the stone, seized possession of the monument, and later disbanded, leaving the construction on hold. Then the Civil War began. In 1876, in celebration of America's 100th birthday, President Ulysses Grant authorized federal funding to finish the monument. Work resumed in 1879. By this time, the plans were outdated, and the obelisk was removed from the plans. An additional issue was after two decades of no work being completed on the monument, matching quarry stone couldn't be found. As a result, the bottom 150 feet of the monument is a different color than the top.

Construction wrapped up in 1884. The capstone, which weighed more than 3,000 pounds, was set in place on December 6, 1884. The project was dedicated the following year but didn't open to the public until 1888. The finished monument stood 555 feet and 5 1/8 inches high, had fifty flights of stairs, and weighed more than 81,000 tons. It was the world's tallest man-made structure until the Eiffel Tower was completed in 1889.

It's so fun to stumble across interesting historical details, especially when I can work them into a story. And this one was such fun to write.

Truthfully, the characters and town of Holiday have captured my heart. I hope you'll continue on the Holiday Express journey by reading *Holiday Heart,* the next book in the series.

Since the Holiday Express line runs from Baker City to Holiday, I wanted to tie in a character or two from my Baker City Brides series. You can read all about Maggie Dalton, her dress shop, and her friends, starting with *Crumpets and Cowpies*.

The mention of a matchmaker in Grass Valley is a little nod to my Grass Valley Brides boxed set. If you haven't yet read it, I promise it is worth the read and full of laughs and swoony romance.

I would be remiss not to express my thanks and gratitude to Katrina, Allison, Alice, Linda, and all the fantastic Hopeless Romantics team for their help in making this book the best it can be. My everlasting gratitude goes out to Josephine Blake, the amazing artist who designed the covers for the series! Thank you, thank you!

Also, my thanks to you, dear reader, for reading Jace and Cora Lee's story. May the love and hope in it reflect the love and hope in your home and heart this holiday season.

Merry Christmas!

Shanna

Thank You

Thank you for reading *Holiday Hope*! I hope you enjoyed the journey of Cora Lee and Jace falling in love. If you did, I'd be so appreciative if you'd consider leaving a review so other readers might discover the book, too.

Holiday Express
Four generations discover the wonder of the season and the magic of one very special train in these sweet holiday romances.
Find them on all Amazon

Also, if you haven't yet signed up for my newsletter, won't you consider subscribing? I send it out when I have new releases, sales, or news of freebies to share. Each month, you can enter a contest, get a new recipe to try, and discover details about upcoming events. When you sign up, you'll receive a free digital book. Don't wait. Sign up today!

Holiday Heart Excerpt

Hearts and humor collide in this sweet holiday romance

Zach Coleman spent his childhood dreaming about trains, and now he's one of the repairmen at the Holiday engine house who keeps them chugging down the tracks. Life couldn't get any sweeter, or so he convinces himself, until he's on his way home from work and saves a woman from getting hit by a wagon. How was he to know that one, brief encounter would upend his world?

Lorna Lennox grew up with the best of everything in life. Her father, a railroad tycoon, has made sure of it. Now that he's moved her into a new house in a remote Oregon location, Lorna wonders if she'll fit into the small community. She's barely arrived in the town of Holiday when an adventure leaves her at the mercy of a handsome stranger. One she finds impossible to forget.

Will the holidays present a chance for hearts to entwine? Find out in this sweet holiday romance rich with history, humor, and the joys of Christmas.

1914

Zach Coleman polished the gilded letters that spelled out "Hope" on the side of a train engine that was as familiar to him as his own hands. His father had been the one to name the engine when it was brand new and had been the first engineer to drive it on the Holiday Express line located in Eastern Oregon.

The steam engine was still running strong, even if his father hadn't driven it in years. Jace Coleman had retired from the railroad shortly after Zach's brother Noah had been born.

Although he thought his father sometimes missed the adventure of driving the train down the tracks between Holiday and Baker City, he knew his parents were happier than most and seemed to cherish each day they had together.

Zach rubbed a brass plaque denoting the company that built the engine and the year it was completed until it shone in the October light streaming in the bank of windows at the engine house, then leaned back to study his handiwork.

"Your dad would be proud," a gravelly voice said from behind him.

He looked over his shoulder at Henry Biggins, the engine house manager and head mechanic. Henry banked the coals in a firebox, preparing the fire to burn all night so the steam engine would be ready to go first thing in the morning.

Growing up, Zach had been crazy about trains and working with his hands. Thanks to his father's training, he'd learned each piece of equipment and part that went on every car of a train from the engine to the caboose. And he'd learned how to tear things apart, study how they operated, then put them back together. Generally, the equipment worked better than it had before he tinkered with it.

He'd been fifteen and desperate to get his hands on a train when Henry had agreed to let him work at the engine house after school. Eight years later, Zach was second in charge and loved his job.

It was hard to imagine how much the small town of Holiday had grown in the last decade. The tiny community had gone from having one hotel, a mercantile, and a few other businesses, to boasting a variety of businesses including four restaurants, three hotels, three general stores, two doctor's offices, and a public school.

Holiday was booming, mostly due to the gold

mine and the mill located north of town. Last month alone, the mill had shipped six hundred carloads of lumber.

Zach had grown up watching the town expand into the bustling community it was today. One of which he was proud to be a resident.

"Is Betty making dumplings for dinner?" Zach asked as he gave the plaque one more rub with the rag in his hand before he jumped off the engine and began to gather his tools.

Henry grinned at him and patted his round belly. "She sure is. I can almost taste them. Mmm, mmm. There's nothing like her dumplings on a fine autumn day."

"Unless it's a nippy winter day." Zach often accompanied Henry home for lunch and enjoyed a hot meal instead of the cold sandwich his mother always packed for him.

"True, my boy. That is true," Henry said as he climbed off the engine and began his nightly routine of checking to make sure everything was turned off, banked, properly stored, and ready for the next day.

Zach used his polishing rag to clean his tools, then hung them on the hooks where they were stored each evening.

Corliss, the seventeen-year-old boy Henry had hired a few weeks ago, pushed the broom across the floor, while Tom, another mechanic who'd worked at the engine house the past three years, locked doors and closed the windows they'd opened earlier since the day had been so warm and pleasant.

"Good job, fellas. Have a nice evening," Henry said, standing at the back door, waiting for them all to exit.

Zach shrugged out of his greasy coveralls, yanked on his cap, tossed his jacket over his shoulder, then pushed his motorcycle outside. He kept it inside the engine house while he was working so no one was tempted to take it for a ride when he wasn't looking. He was the only one in town who rode one, although one of the Milton boys had been considering a purchase of a Harley Davidson. Personally, Zach preferred the Henderson model he rode but figured Andy Milton could make up his own mind about what he wanted.

"Does your mother still grimace every time you ride that thing to town?" Henry asked as Zach draped his jacket over the handlebars of the motorcycle.

"Every time."

Henry chuckled. "Cora Lee just worries about her boys. It's a wonder your sweet mama's hair hasn't turned white after raising you three hooligans."

Zach feigned an affronted look. "Jonah's the rabble-rouser. Noah's the hooligan. I'm the fair-haired child who's never done anything wrong."

The sound of Henry's laughter echoed around them as they sauntered away from the depot.

"Fair-haired child? Now that's a good one, Zach. Considering your hair is nearly black and you were, and sometimes still are, full of more mischief than the other two put together, that is a comment worth a laugh. You may have been sneakier about being caught than your brothers and gotten away with more shenanigans since you were the youngest, but you are every bit as ornery as Jonah and Noah. Every bit."

Zach shrugged and grinned at Henry when they came to an intersection and waited for a wagon headed for the express office to drive by. "Tell Betty I said hello."

"Will do. Give your folks my best regards." Henry tipped his head to Zach, then sauntered north in the direction of the tidy little cottage where he and his wife lived.

Still grinning, Zach continued to push his motorcycle through the intersection rather than riding it, since the noise it made always drew a lot of attention and interest he didn't particularly appreciate receiving. His mother had asked him to bring home cinnamon and nutmeg for her baking, so he headed toward Roger's Mercantile. His family had been shopping there since the store had opened back in the years before Holiday had been incorporated as a town. Rupert Rogers had made money in gold mining. He used the funds to build the store and purchase stock. Then he'd married a woman named Goldie, and they'd raised a son and two daughters in the apartment above the store. As the town had grown, so had the success of the mercantile. Even with other stores in town, Roger's Mercantile remained the largest and most successful. Five years ago, Rupert had retired, and he and Goldie had moved to Portland to live near their daughters. Their son, Albert, and his wife, Helen, had taken over the store, guiding it on to more success while maintaining the friendly service so many in Holiday had come to expect.

Thoughts of the delicious baked goods his mother was sure to create with the spices and the baskets of apples he'd recently helped pick made his mouth water as he neared the town's park that had been installed two years ago.

Pathways lined with crushed gravel, artfully planted rosebushes and shrubs, and even a fountain where children splashed during the summer heat made the park a wonderful place to visit. A magnificent gazebo, the likes of which no one had seen in these parts until it had been constructed, stood in the center of the park, a testament to Holiday's growth. His father had been the one to suggest the design, based on a similar gazebo he'd once seen in his travels back East when he'd been an engineer.

Zach slowed his step and studied the gazebo as he pushed his motorcycle toward the mercantile located across the town's main street.

Painted white, the gazebo had been constructed in an octagon shape with eight sturdy pillars encircling it. The foundation was made of brick hauled up from Baker City. Between three pillars on each side, there were built-in flower boxes that burst with a profusion of flowers from spring through the autumn season, thanks to the efforts of the Holiday Women's League, of which his mother was a founding member. The north and south ends of the gazebo were left open for people to wander through, while benches lined the inside of the gazebo, inviting people to sit and rest. Lattice work hung along the eaves, beneath the unique bell-shaped copper roof topped with a beautiful cupola.

Arched dormers centered between the pillars always made him think of a woman's petticoats flouncing out in a scalloped ripple as she spun across a dance floor.

Amused by his fanciful thoughts, he stopped and stared at a young woman as she studied the gazebo. Sunlight danced across her bare head, making it look as though the chestnut tresses glowed with bright embers. The dark green dress she wore perfectly fit her curvaceous form. Even from a distance, he could almost feel the energy pulsing off her as she held her hands in front of her, index fingers and thumbs positioned to make an imaginary picture frame. She tilted her head in study and continued backing up. If she'd held a camera in her hands, he would have thought she was a photographer, aligning her photograph before she captured the image.

As it was, if she didn't stop, she was likely to back right into the street and get hit by a passing automobile or wagon. Surely, she was aware of how close she was to danger.

But as she continued moving away from the gazebo, one step at a time, Zach hastily rocked his motorcycle onto the rear kickstand and took off running across the park. He hoped to reach her before she injured herself.

"Miss!" he shouted, but the woman paid him no heed as she continued edging backward. Zach glanced behind her to the street. Doc Holt drove his Model T toward her at a rapid pace while a wagon full of lumber jostled directly for her from the opposite direction.

"Miss!" he yelled louder, sprinting toward her as she stepped into the street, seemingly oblivious to the world around her.

Zach lunged forward, grabbed her around the waist, and swung around with such force, it knocked them both to the ground, a mere foot away from the wheels of the hulking lumber wagon as it rolled past them.

"Nice catch, Zach!" Ernie Elroy yelled from the wagon seat as he continued on his way. "No wonder you're so good at baseball."

Air stirred against Zach's cheek as the woman beneath him drew in a startled gasp. A soft fragrance enveloped him, a scent of delicate flowers mixed with something rich and sensual. The only word that came to mind to describe the perfume was scrumptious, and that was not a word he'd even known was in his vocabulary.

Time slowed until it nearly stood still as the woman shifted slightly. Zach became acutely aware of how well her curves, so soft and lush, fit against the angles and planes of his body as he held her wrapped in his arms. He could feel the runaway thumping of her heart as it kept time with the wildly beating tempo in his chest.

Despite how improper it was for him to be pressed against a woman he'd never met, he couldn't force himself to move away. Instead, he placed his hands flat on either side of her and pushed himself up far enough to look into her face.

A wild tumble of curls that had escaped her hairpins fell around her forehead and down to her shoulders. One springy coil rested on her cheek.

Zach gently lifted it away, rubbing the silky strands between his fingers before he tucked it behind her ear. He took in a complexion his mother would have referred to as peaches and cream, even if it was dotted by freckles across her cheeks, and a thin, small nose. He noticed a scar above her left eyebrow, and a tiny, barely noticeable dimple in her stubborn chin.

Lips that did, indeed, remind him of ripe peaches, made him wonder if they'd taste as sweet. The woman's heart-shaped face gave her the appearance of a mischievous pixie. But it was her eyes that held and captivated him. He'd never seen eyes such a pale shade of green, like frost had settled over the heart of a forest glade. Unlike a frozen landscape, though, they held warmth. A great deal of warmth, and, if he wasn't mistaken, a bit of humor.

The lovely young woman was unlike any he'd ever encountered. He hesitated to end this most unexpected encounter with her, doubting he'd have a second opportunity to be this close to such a fascinating female. Unable to stop himself, he allowed his head to dip closer to her, inhaling again her luscious scent.

"Hi," he whispered, unsure why he felt the need to speak so quietly, other than to keep from breaking the spell she had seemingly cast over him.

"Hi," she replied in a hushed tone. The barest hint of a smile kicked up the right corner of her mouth, making him battle the urge to kiss her tempting lips. "Thank you for rescuing me."

"My pleasure," he said, reluctantly pushing

himself off her, rolling to the side, and rising to his feet. He extended both hands to her and, when she clasped them, pulled her upright. Propriety demanded he immediately turn loose of her fingers, but he couldn't muster the will to let her go.

"I do apologize for not paying better attention." The smile she offered to him showed off teeth so white they nearly dazzled him in spite of a front tooth being slightly crooked. She tugged one hand free from his and waved it in the direction of the gazebo. "That is the most spectacular gazebo I've ever seen. I was picturing how best to draw it and got lost in my thoughts. Just when I'd landed on the precise perfection of placement, the vision changed. It's a dilly! What a sight to behold when the sun began to dip toward the horizon and sent beams of gold dancing off that glorious copper roof. Just take a gander and see if it doesn't leave you mesmerized."

Something had left him mesmerized, for certain, and it had nothing to do with the sunset or the gazebo. He tried to yank his scattered wits together long enough to extract at least one thread of conversation. "You're an artist?"

She laughed, not a silly schoolgirl laugh, but one that held the confidence of a woman. "No. I lack the talent and dedication to be an artist, but I do enjoy sketching and sometimes add splashes of color to my endeavors."

Zach realized people were staring at them and released the woman's hand before someone he knew marched over and began asking questions. His mother, sister-in-law, and all the females in the

Milton family felt it was their duty to constantly be on the lookout for his potential bride.

The problem was that Zach was perfectly happy with his life the way it was. His father and grandfather had both assured him, when the right woman came along, he'd change his perspective on remaining blissfully single. Until she did, he had no intention of letting the women in his life force him into courting a girl he had no interest in pursuing. A fact that he'd reiterated frequently, even if no one listened to him.

As he studied the woman beside him, he felt something shift inside him, as though it was a moment of great importance, one he'd always remember.

"I hope I didn't hurt you." Zach knew he'd probably landed on her rather hard, but that was preferable to the woman being run over by Ernie's lumber wagon. As he looked at her, though, with the sunlight setting her hair aflame and her eyes sparkling with interest, she certainly appeared unharmed. And far too pretty for his jangled nerves to ignore.

She shook her head, causing all that wondrous hair to shimmer in the fading light. For a wickedly decadent minute, he considered how hard she might slap him if he yielded to the ever-increasing need to kiss her. Lest the desire overtake him, he took a step back. "You're sure you aren't hurt?"

"No. I'm fine, sir, and your assistance in keeping me from being seriously injured due to my negligence is appreciated." She brushed at the back of her skirt, then turned those uniquely beautiful eyes on him. "Truly, I'm grateful for your help."

"My pleasure, Miss …"

"Lennox. Lorna Lennox. I arrived in town earlier this afternoon and wanted to explore a bit before dinner. I'd barely started on my walk when I happened to see the gazebo."

"It's nice to meet you, Miss Lennox. Welcome to Holiday. I'm Zach Coleman."

"Coleman? If I have my details in order, your family has been here since before Holiday became a town."

He grinned. "That's true. Pops—he's my grandfather—moved out here when my father and uncle were young. We've been living out at Elk Creek Ranch ever since."

"Your father and uncle live there now? With your grandfather?"

Zach wanted to sidestep her question, but if she asked anyone about their family, everyone in town seemed to know the story of his uncle Jude. Might as well tell her the truth and see how she reacted to it. Over the years, he'd found the reactions of people to be a good gauge of their character.

"My father runs the ranch. My brother Noah will take over when Dad decides to slow down. Pops lives in a little house on the ranch with his wife, Ava. They married about ten years ago, and we call her Grams. As for my uncle, he died in prison when I was three."

"Oh, I'm sorry to hear about your uncle." Lorna placed a hand over his and offered a sympathetic squeeze. "But it's marvelous the rest of your family is there."

"Not quite all of my family. My oldest brother, Jonah, moved to Idaho where he and his wife ranch with her parents."

"Do you have other siblings, besides the two brothers you mentioned?"

Zach smirked. "Nope. I'm not sure my folks could have kept up with more of us. They claim Jonah, Noah, and I were a handful."

She smiled again. Zach entertained the crazy notion that it was like having sunlight poured directly into his soul.

"I imagine you were a handful," she said, "but I believe children with a little gumption are tomorrow's future."

"Then the future of Holiday is secure because I grew up with a gang of troublemakers." Zach leaned closer to her and dropped his voice. "Sadly, most of them have matured past such nonsense."

"That's both gladdening and disheartening to hear."

Before Zach could decipher what she meant, she brushed at her skirts one more time, then gave him a long glance. "I do thank you for saving me from a premature demise at the wheels of that hulking wagon."

"I'm more than happy to be of assistance. Since you are so new to town, would it be acceptable if I walk you home, just to make sure you arrive there safely?"

"Under the circumstances, I suppose that would be more than acceptable." She took a step toward the street, then looked down as though she'd just noticed the planks that covered the entire main street from a block past the church to the other end of town just beyond the marshal's office and jail.

The board-covered street was a source of pride in Holiday. When it rained, the boards kept the street from becoming a quagmire. In the summer, it helped keep down the dust. Zach had heard from his uncle R.C. that the town hoped to place boards on several more streets in the spring. As one of the town's councilmen, R.C. was usually in the know when it came to happenings in Holiday.

Zach motioned toward the motorcycle he'd left on the other side of the park. "I'll be right back," he said, loping back to where he'd left the Henderson, then pushed it up the street and around the corner to where Lorna waited.

"Is it not in an operable state?"

"Oh, it works just fine, but I try not to use it too much in town." He looked both ways before pushing the bike into the street. They crossed to the other side in front of the mercantile. He waved at Albert Rogers as he carried a box out and loaded it in old Mrs. Piedmont's automobile. She and her husband had owned the hotel in town for years, but they'd sold it last spring to a young couple who'd come west from Virginia. The Kindalls were nice people, and the hotel seemed to be doing well.

"Why don't you ride it in town?" Lorna turned to the right and continued walking, although she darted several glances at him.

"Some of the women folk think it's too noisy, and some of the kids come running as soon as they hear it, wanting a ride."

A teasing smile lifted her lips upward. "The

children have the right idea. I think it would be a dandy treat to ride such a machine."

"Maybe one day I'll give you a ride, if you'd like."

Lorna clasped her hands beneath her chin and beamed at him. "I'd like that very much!"

"We'll plan on it, then. Soon. In a few weeks, it will likely start to snow, and I'll have to ride a horse to town instead of this." Zach tipped his head toward the motorcycle, then looked back at her as they headed south on Holiday's Main Street. "Where do you live?"

"Our house is on Mulberry Lane, just off Milton Road."

Zach had no idea where Mulberry Lane was, but he was familiar with Milton Road. He'd spent hours and hours playing with the Milton family, for whom the street was named. Even though they weren't related, he considered R.C. and Anne Milton his uncle and aunt, and their bevy of children his cousins.

"Is it a new house?" Zach asked as they continued past the bank, then crossed the street and headed past the telephone office and a newly opened restaurant. Charles Milton and his wife, Susan, had eaten there the other day and raved about the food.

"Yes and no. It's been a project my father has worked on for a while, but he finished it in July. It just took a while for us to move everything here from our home in Philadelphia."

"I'm sure it's quite a change being here in Holiday compared to a big city like that." He couldn't begin to imagine how the small community measured up to a bustling city, but there wasn't anywhere he'd rather be than Holiday. It was home to him and always would be.

"It is a change, but I think I'm going to like it here. It's so peaceful and quiet, and the air smells like Christmas." Lorna closed her eyes and inhaled deeply, drawing Zach's attention to her curvy figure before he glanced away.

"Funny you should mention Christmas. Our little town loves the Christmas season, and you won't find anyone who enjoys it more than my mother. She starts baking right after Thanksgiving. The men in my family do our best to eat everything as fast as she pulls it out of the oven."

Lorna laughed. "I'm picturing you and your brothers, father, and grandfather all poised around the oven, waiting for a tray of cookies fresh from the oven."

"It's happened before. If you don't believe me, ask Mamie."

"Mamie? Who's that?" Lorna's brow wrinkled slightly in confusion.

"My mother. We call her Mamie. When Jonah was little, he heard people calling her Cora Lee—that's her name, you see. He knew she was his mama, so he combined it all together and the name Mamie stuck. Even the Milton bunch refers to her as Mamie now."

"Milton bunch? As in Milton Road?"

Zach nodded as they reached a crossroads. The large Milton Feed and Seed building sitting diagonally across the street housed not just a feedstore, but also a blacksmith shop, livery, and auto repair business. R.C. had purchased half a section of land not long after he and Anne had wed. The feed store was located on the end of the property nearest town. A pasture where they kept cows and horses separated it from the farmhouse and three-story barn R.C. and Anne had built a dozen years ago.

He pointed to the feedstore. "Milton Feed and Seed. Everything you need for caring for animals large and small, raising a garden, maintaining an automobile, renting a horse and buggy, getting a horse shod, or having metal work completed. It's also the livery and blacksmith shop."

"Quite an enterprise," Lorna said, studying the building, then pointing down the road to the house and barn in the distance. "Is that another cupola?"

"On the barn. I'll ask Uncle R.C. if I can show it to you sometime. The barn has a big arena inside where the Milton boys show off their roping and riding skills. There's a set of steps inside that go up to the cupola, and the widow's walk has the best view around these parts."

"I'm sure it is something to see and shall look forward to exploring it at the convenience of your uncle." She appeared baffled as she turned to the left and started up Milton Road. "How are you related to the Milton family?"

"I'm not, by blood, but we spent so much time around them when we were all little, they became our aunt and uncle like my parents are to their children. There are ten of them."

"Ten children?"

"Yep. They had six boys, three girls, and then Timothy, who was a bit of a surprise to Aunt Anne. She thought she was through having children when he came along."

"I'm sure he's a special blessing to them."

Zach chuckled. "I'm not positive Uncle R.C. would describe him that way, but it's a nice thought."

He glanced ahead of him and saw the newly constructed mansion owned by the railroad tycoon. The man had arrived in Holiday and started buying up trains and investing in mines, and had even bought a partnership in the lumber mill. Suddenly, Lorna's last name penetrated the fog that had descended on his brain the moment he'd seen her gazing at the gazebo.

"You're *that* Lennox? You're related to George Lennox?" Stunned, he stopped outside the wrought iron fence encompassing a yard that appeared to be acres in size. Everything about the yard looked precise and purposefully arranged, much like the imposing three-story brick house where Lorna now resided.

She turned to him and smiled. "Yes. George is my father. Do you know him?"

Zach couldn't tell her he'd only seen Mr. Lennox from a distance, or that he'd heard Henry complaining about the demanding, sometimes exasperating man who barked out orders and expected each one to be obeyed immediately. If rumors proved true, George Lennox was eccentric, irritable, and rich enough to buy anything he wanted or desired including the entire town of Holiday.

"I've not yet had the pleasure of meeting him," Zach said, doing his best to sound casual instead of on guard. Of course, it stood to reason the first woman to truly stir his interest had to be the daughter of a man with more money than kindness or common sense.

"Papa isn't home now, but I'll introduce you another day."

Zach highly doubted her father would allow her to consort with the likes of him, but kept his opinions to himself.

"I reckon I better head for home. Again, welcome to Holiday, Miss Lennox. In the future, you might want to be more careful about where you're walking. I'd hate to see you get hurt while you're planning the next picture you'll draw."

"Thank you, Mr. Coleman. I shall endeavor to be more aware of my surroundings. Would you care to come in for some refreshments before you venture to your home?" She pushed open the gate on the walk, then turned and gave him such a warm smile, Zach took a few steps forward before he stopped himself.

No good could possibly come from fraternizing with the daughter of the man who essentially owned the railroad, and could therefore fire him on a whim. Despite how much he wanted to spend time with Lorna, he had to turn her down.

"Maybe another time, Miss Lennox. I promised Mamie I'd run by the store and pick up some spices for her baking. I'd best get to it before the mercantile closes."

"My apologies for detaining you, sir. My

deepest gratitude to you, again, for rescuing me and ensuring I made it safely home."

"You're welcome." Zach touched his fingers to his cap and turned his bike around, ready to leave. He'd only taken three steps when he stopped and glanced back over his shoulder to see Lorna watching him. "I don't know if you've heard or are even interested, but the community is holding a festival to celebrate Halloween and the end of harvest. It's this Saturday at the Grange Hall. You'll find it across the street from the church, next to the school on the other end of town. It's a costume party, so you can dress up if you like, but you don't have to."

"Oh, it sounds perfect! Thank you for the invitation. Perhaps I'll see you there."

"I'll be there." Zach grinned at her and hopped on his bike, starting it up and roaring down the street.

As he headed to the mercantile, he envisioned the type of costume Miss Lorna Lennox, heir to the Lennox empire, might wear. In spite of the voice in his head warning him to stay far away from the girl, he was glad he'd happened upon her at the park. He looked forward to seeing her again Saturday at the party.

Available on Amazon

About the Author

PHOTO BY SHANA BAILEY PHOTOGRAPHY

USA Today bestselling author Shanna Hatfield is a farm girl who loves to write. Her sweet historical and contemporary romances are filled with sarcasm, humor, hope, and hunky heroes.

When Shanna isn't dreaming up unforgettable characters, twisting plots, or covertly seeking dark, decadent chocolate, she hangs out with her beloved husband, Captain Cavedweller, at their home in the Pacific Northwest.

Shanna loves to hear from readers. Connect with her online:

Blog: shannahatfield.com
Facebook: Shanna Hatfield's Page
Shanna Hatfield's Hopeless Romantics Group
Pinterest: Shanna Hatfield
Email: shanna@shannahatfield.com

Made in the USA
Columbia, SC
29 November 2021